DIASPORA

DIASPORA

NEW WORLD ADVENTURES

J.P. Ozuna

ISBN: 979-8-9866698-2-3 (print)
ISBN: 979-8-9866698-3-0 (ebook)

Book design by Wordzworth
www.wordzworth.com

Cover design by Getcovers

Published by Platano Publishing
www.platanopublishing.com

CONTENTS

Acknowledgments   vii

Episode One   1

Episode Two   12

Episode Three   23

Episode Four   35

Episode Five   46

Episode Six   59

Episode Seven   71

Episode Eight   82

Episode Nine   93

Episode Ten   103

Episode Eleven   113

Episode Twelve   122

Episode Thirteen   132

Episode Fourteen   142

Episode Fifteen   153

About The Author   165

ACKNOWLEDGMENTS

I want to first acknowledge you, the reader, for choosing this book and allowing me to entertain you. I appreciate you and hope this story can impact you in meaningful ways.

Thank you to my editor and those who continue to support me on this journey. Especially:

Rosalin Ozuna, without you, this would not have been possible.

Derek Bruno, your unconditional support has been invaluable.

Author Benjamin Burgess, words cannot express my appreciation. Thank you for your continued support.

Johanna Lamarche, thank you for believing in this dream and joining me on this adventure.

Thank you to my loving and supportive family, especially: Angeline Ozuna, Leodith Valdez, Michelle Hernandez, John Bourdierd, Melissa Bobadilla, Maria Regalado, and everyone else. You are too many to name. Know that I love and appreciate every single one of you.

I am forever grateful to my friends for your love and unconditional support and to everyone who has supported 2030. Thank you.

My beloved children inspire and motivate me to follow my dreams. Nathaniel Lopez, Jade Bruno, and Anisha Bruno. I love you.

Finally, I want to dedicate this beautiful story to my nieces and nephews. Angel Ozuna, Luis Ozuna, Eddy Valverde, Edelyn Valverde, Chalyn Rodriguez, and Crystal Lehrer.

EPISODE ONE

The air in the ship is thin. I can't get enough to fill my lungs, and it hurts to breathe. It smells foul of vomit, feces, and urine. I'm bleeding, unsure where it's coming from. Mucus is falling from my nose, and my eyes burn. I have no tears left, and my back aches.

I can't sit upright because there is no space, and the chains cut into my skin. The ship is rocking forcibly, and the motion makes me ill. I've lost track of time, and though I've called upon death to free me from this ara,[1] it has yet to come. I envy those whose emi[2] have left their bodies. The body can only endure so much, but the ori[3] is eternal, and now they rest with Olodumare.[4]

I cry in anguish and feel a sharp pain pierce my side as some bastard brutally kicks me.

Camila sat up, gasping for air. Those dreams are recurring, and she prays every night for them to stop. They cease for a while but always return. She told no one about them, not even her best friend in the world, Gaby, nor her parents. They disturb her because she doesn't recognize herself in them, the time, or the place. They seem ancient, and she doesn't understand what they mean.

My name is Idelfonsa Perez. I am forty-five years old and of Yoruba descent, from Cuba. I own a botanica in Yonkers, New York. It

---

[1]   Body
[2]   Spirit
[3]   Soul
[4]   The Yoruba believe that the ori is given to a person by Olodumare, Supreme Being or God, before a person is born, and returns to Olodumare at death.

belonged to my parents before me, and our family home is directly above. The new generation comes to my botanica to buy palo santo, sage, evil eye pendants, and other trinkets. My older customers come in for divination, potions, and to consult the spirit realm.

Today, I have two of my favorite regulars, a pair of best friends connected by more than friendship. Gabriela Hernandez, whose parents are Afro Colombian, from Cartagena, Colombia, and Camila De Los Santos, whose parents are from San Pedro de Macorís, Dominican Republic. They are both of Yoruba lineage but are unaware of it. Especially the Dominican girl. The Dominicans rarely acknowledge their African heritage in her culture. It doesn't matter how dark their skin is; they'll claim everything else under the sun, but … The Taínos were the unfortunate victims of genocide. The Dominicans will identify with the Spanish, French, Middle Eastern—anyone *but* the enslaved Africans.

They colloquially call the descendants of enslaved Africans *cocolos*[5] that migrated to the island and settled in San Pedro de Macorís and La Romana from the neighboring islands, like St. Kitts and Nevis, Leeward Islands, Virgin Islands, Anguilla, and Antigua, as if they don't share the same African ancestry.

Camila didn't know that during the ten-year war, Cuban sugar planters and their enslaved people had fled to the Dominican Republic, searching for new lands and security from the insurrection.

Slavery was abolished and outlawed internationally in 1806. However, it took another eighty years before enslaved people were finally free in Cuba in 1886.

Sadly, many slave ships sailed to Cuba from Africa, while Harriet Tubman courageously freed enslaved people in America with the underground railroad.

Camila's Yoruba heritage comes from those Cubans that settled in the Dominican Republic. Still, Hispaniola[6] was the first Spanish colony and among the first to enslave people from Africa, way back in the 1500s. Hence, enslaved people had already been on that island for three hundred years.

---

[5] Term used in the Hispanic Caribbean to refer to Afro Caribbean migrant descendants, specifically, Anglophone immigrants.

[6] What the Spanish colonists called present-day Haiti/Dominican Republic.

Anyway, enough with the history lesson. Through no fault of her own, what I'm getting at is that the ancestral tug is strong. It pulls your heartstrings unceasingly. Drum vibrations are felt with each heartbeat, the call of the ancestors in every pump, their blood in our blood.

Although they were whipped and burned, raped and maimed, ripped and torn, the connection is deep, and the bond is strong. Despite being beaten into accepting the master's God, they hid their true devotion behind their saints like Lucumí, my friend's secret.

A people oppressed, exploited, and terrorized, cannot trust the justice of a God that condones it. So, unconsciously, they now seek what they do not understand, ignorant of things they don't know.

The enslaved people arrived later in Cuba, so the voyage is still consciously fresh for some of us. So, naturally, we did not accept the new God. Instead, we continued to practice our faith, and regardless of the outcome or how far and wide the enslaved Yoruba reached, our ancestors' will forever remain imprinted in our souls.

We were called savage for our animal sacrifices, but didn't they sacrifice animals to their God? Didn't they kill for their God? Didn't they rape, pillage, and plunder for their God? How can their God be better if the behavior was the same—or worse?

So many of us have filled ourselves with hatred and resentment, poisoning our spirit. However, we must move forward and look to the future with love, loving ourselves first. This story isn't about my faith or their ignorance. It's about how enslaved Africans were brought to a new world, making it their own.

Despite how desperately they tried to eradicate our power by calling it evil, it is still within us, and what our ancestors endured will have been worth it the day we rediscover it.

Camila and Gaby feel a strong connection, so they are best friends, but they don't understand why. I'll tell you why. Unbeknownst to them, they share a common ancestor, Iyayun. She was the beloved of Yoruba King Aganju. His reign was long and very prosperous.

Toward the end of his reign, he waged war with a namesake of his, Aganju the Onisambo, for refusing him the hand of his daughter Iyayun. In this war, many died, their towns destroyed, and the bride forcibly secured.

Significant domestic troubles clouded the end of King Aganju's reign. His only son, Lubegò, was discovered to have an illicit relationship with King Aganju's beloved Iyayun. On Iyayun's account, many princes and people lost their lives.[7]

Camila and Gabriela are direct descendants of Iyayun. That's why they have such a strong bond. But here's the kicker. The girls have boyfriends, twins, Thiago and Paulo Silva. They are also of Yoruba ancestry from Brazil.

What are the odds, you're probably asking yourself? But the Universe works in mysterious, synchronistic ways, and we cannot escape our *kadara*.[8]

Those connected to us always gravitate into our lives despite time and space. The boys are similar in many respects, but they are very different. They are twins but are not identical.

Thiago is tall with beautiful mocha skin, black, curly hair, and dimples when he smiles. Paulo is shorter, with a tawny complexion and coarse auburn hair. Both are handsome and charming in their own way. They play soccer, so they have lean, muscular bodies and strong legs.

The girls look more like twins if you ask me. They are majestic goddesses of striking beauty, with cinnamon skin tones and hickory, almond-shaped eyes. They are full of life and have profoundly expressive and voluptuous lips. In addition, they have curvy, athletic figures that turn heads.

Gabriela has beautiful, tight curls, and Camila interchanges between curly and straight. You have to give it to the Dominican hairdressers. They can straighten any natural hair and handle those blow-dryers like lethal weapons.

The girls often come for small trinkets and their sage, but I suspect they are fond of me. Pardon my presumption, but I call it as I see it; perception is my gift.

Gabriela had a new look, a freshly shaved, bleached head with colorful eyeshadow, bright red lips, and a long-sleeve black crop top with jeans and a matching denim jacket.

"Nice haircut," I said.

---

[7] *The History of the Yorubas*, book by Samuel Johnson.
[8] Destiny

"Thank you," she said with a big smile. "It's my middle finger to the patriarchy." She added to this by showing me her middle finger.

I love young people on a quest to find themselves. They keep the world interesting.

Camila is pensive and preoccupied with her thoughts. Nevertheless, she looked comfy in a matching lavender sweatsuit with black Converse sneakers.

"You didn't get much sleep," I said.

"How did you know?" Camila asked me shadily as she petted Midnight, my cat, as she rubbed her cheeks against Camila's leg.

"You look tired," I replied, stating the obvious.

"Oh, just a bad dream," she told me. I looked at her to see and told her she gets them often.

"I wish my mom would let me have a cat. By the way, do you have sexy perfume oils?" she inquired, changing the subject and picking up Midnight in her arms.

"What's the occasion?" I asked with curiosity, and she blushed.

Sexy perfume oils are a first, and Gabriela filled me in. It's senior year, and it's time to lose their virginity, but before prom, as Gaby said, making a face, "Losing your virginity the night of prom is so cliché!"

I laughed because we often cease to make things memorable for fear that they may be "cliché," but avoiding a cliché is the same thing in and of itself.

"Those *Ibeyi*[9] are lucky," I said between cackles, and Midnight jumped out of Camila's arms, disappearing.

"Those what?" Camila asked, not understanding, sitting on a stool by the counter.

"The twins," I said. These girls always make me laugh. "*Los Ibeyi, con las dos Aguas!*"[10] I said to myself, referring to the sweet waters and salt waters of the two Yoruba deities, Oshun and Yemaya.

They stared at me. Hispanic kids barely speak Spanish these days. "Don't mind me, girls. I have some patchouli for your special night. You won't need anything else!"

---

[9]   The twins
[10] With the two waters

I've concocted many love potions in my day and have found that love is the best aphrodisiac, and no number of potions or spells can ever duplicate or mimic its effects.

Although you can see love when it is there, its absence is most noticeable, and I know, without a doubt, that those kids are in love.

Love is all they'll need, but this isn't a love story, either. Instead, this is a story of self-discovery and adventure, so be patient. *Ori mi a sin o lo,*[11] I said as they left my shop.

So much excitement to come; the girls go as children and will return to me as women, full of power but needing guidance.

Thiago and Paulo have the house to themselves. "You two coming over after school?" Thiago asked, placing his arm around Camila's shoulders.

"Our parents are going to Atlantic City for the weekend!" Paulo added, holding Gabriela's hand.

They met up with the girls before their next class. The crowded hallway was full of students standing around or rushing to the next destination. Chatter filled the air as the late bell rang.

"Come on; we're going to make feijoada.[12] You both will love it," said Thiago, enticing them with food. Those girls love to eat, and they will try anything.

"With some white rice," Paulo emphasized, knowing Camila loved rice, and it was harder to convince her because her mother was super strict.

"Sounds good," the girls said in unison. They do that often.

"I need to have the white rice with it," Camila added with a smile, and they walked down the hall like they were not already late.

"Let's go, you four. Get to your next class!" the assistant principal barked, walking by them. Most of the other students were in class, and the second late bell had already rung.

"Thank God we're almost out of here!" Gaby said happily.

"Friday, finally," they said to each other when the school day was over. The twins had a car, given to them on their sixteenth birthday by their parents, and they all got in. It was a beautiful spring day.

---

[11]   May my *orisha* guide you and bless you
[12]   A popular Brazilian dish, a stew of beans with beef and pork. It is widely believed the beginning of feijoada stem from slavery in Brazil.

The sun was shining, the flowers were blooming, the air was warm, and they were a day closer to graduation, which they all anticipated with excitement.

Class of 2012! It's as if the yellow school bus was dropping them off for their first day of high school yesterday. All the first-year students nervously arrived, hoping high school wouldn't be as frightening as they felt.

Camila and Gaby had each other and confidently got off the bus. The boys also rode the same bus and were immediately captivated by them.

Thiago and Paulo were spellbound when the bus stopped, and Camila and Gabriela walked in as if they had fallen from heaven.

Camila and Gaby attended a private school for their elementary and middle years, so they didn't know anyone.

The girls called home to say they'd be staying late at school, and Camila's mom mentioned, "*El novio ése.*"[13] She told Camila she didn't want "*una barriga en está casa.*"[14] Then warned her that she was no fool. "*Cuando tu ibas, yo venía!*"[15] she finally said, and Camila ended the call.

"Seventeen, and she still treats me like a child, making a big deal about everything," Camila told the others, and they poked fun at her and laughed.

Camila had missed out on many outings, trips, and other events because of her mother's firm parenting style.

Her mother has always been strict and never allowed Camila to attend sleepovers next door at Gabriela's.

"She made a good point, though," Camila said in deep thought.

"Doesn't she always? What did she say now?" Gabriela asked.

"She doesn't want no grandkids, that's for sure," Camila said, laughing.

They all lived in Yonkers, New York. My botanica is close to the high school they attended. Camila and Gabriela are next-door neighbors and have known each other since childhood. Their fathers own a moving company, Caby Movers. The men have been friends since they were in college.

---

[13] That boyfriend
[14] A pregnancy in the house
[15] I've been around longer than you

They met the girls' mothers while attending college and started making moves on rented U-Haul trucks until they finally purchased a moving truck of their own and then another.

"You two have condoms?" Gabriela asked unceremoniously, and Camila slapped her arm.

"Damn, girl, nothing subtle about you, is there?" she asked jokingly.

The boys had tensed up with Gaby's question, but they all laughed now that Camila had lightened the mood.

"Anyway, have either of you ever had sex before?" Gabriel continued, killing the mood again, and Camila slapped her forehead with her palm in disbelief.

"Yes, of course!" Paulo exclaimed, and Gabriela raised her brows with skepticism.

"Really? When? Because we've known each other since ninth grade, and you haven't dated anyone but me, and if you say middle school, I want to know her name," she said, pointing at Paulo.

There was a long pause. "Well?" Gabriela pressed, anxious for the details, and Camila shook her head. The girl had no filter and said things precisely as she thought them.

Camila, on the other hand, was more diplomatic and reserved. She was very considerate of other people's feelings and often disregarded what she wanted to avoid regarding the conflict.

"It was the summer after ninth grade when we went on vacation to Brazil. Our cousin Juliana had a lot of friends, and since we spent the entire summer there, we got to know some very nice girls," Paulo said.

"Oh, OK." Gabriela sighed.

I always told the girls not to ask questions if they were not ready for the answer, but, of course, he was lying. They had been saving themselves for the girls who stole their hearts in ninth grade, and their patience was about to pay off big time.

"I'll stop at the pharmacy. Is there anything else either of you needs? You know, to make it more comfortable," Thiago asked with grave concern.

Camila smiled at him. "It's not that serious, babe. We will all figure this out together. I know you guys are 'experienced,' but your Brazilian sexcapades were a lifetime ago."

Camila winked at Thiago, who said, "I love you."

Then Paulo and Gabriela yucked and ew'd in symphony before Camila could answer, and Thiago exited the school parking lot laughing.

Gabriela and Paulo thought Camila and Thiago were too "lovey-dovey," too intense, and they're more lighthearted and goofy, so they can't relate.

"Yes, Romeo, let's get this show on the road. You have food to cook and cherries to pop," Gaby prompted him.

They all erupted with laughter again. Gaby was blunt and funny, the certified group clown, with Paulo a close second.

Once home, Thiago and Paulo got started in the kitchen. It was a lovely eat-in kitchen with cherry oak cabinets and a center island. The girls sat to watch them cook, teasing and showering them with compliments.

Of course, Camila took Pelé, the Brazilian terrier and Silvas' family pet, into her arms and gave him a tight hug as he licked the side of her face.

"Hey, Mr. Steal, don't kiss my lady," Thiago said to the dog.

"I like him better," Camila teased.

"I know you do," Thiago said, blowing her a kiss.

"You ladies want a beer?" Paulo asked, and Thiago frowned.

"Yes!" they exclaimed simultaneously.

Camila and Gaby giggled, full of excitement and anticipation.

Thiago turned from the stove to face them. "Really? Underage drinking? Camila, not only will I send you home deflowered, but drunk too?"

Paulo and the girls burst into laughter at his seriousness again.

"Seriously, bro?" Paulo asked, opening the two-door refrigerator and taking out beers for all.

"You need a shot of tequila!" Paulo said to Thiago. "You're too uptight."

Thiago has an old soul. That boy was from another time. He was very proper, the sort of gentleman the likes of which we no longer see.

They ate, and Camila asked for seconds. "So good!" she exclaimed, delighted. "Thanks for making the rice. Dominicans eat rice with everything," she said, digging in a second time. That girl can eat.

After eating, they moved to the spacious living room furnished with a brown microfiber sectional, coffee table, TV stand, and a beautiful multicolored area rug.

They sat cuddling with another round of beers and were satisfied with all they had to eat. The boys were good cooks, and although the girls tried, they couldn't cook to save their lives.

Gaby played music, and they all sang about remaining forever young and setting the world ablaze.

It is wonderful to be young, wild, and free. Of course, I wouldn't go back to my youth if my life depended on it, but it is important to enjoy it while you have it.

Another song came on, and Gaby jumped out of her seat, using her cell phone as a microphone. She pulled Camila off the sofa, and they danced while the boys watched, enthralled. The boys were lucky because the girls were beautiful. They smiled as they watched the dancers.

Gaby wore a short denim skirt, brown knee-high boots, and a multicolored striped blouse. Camila wore a gray V-neck shirt, blue jeans, and black ankle boots.

Then "Dutty Love" came on, and Gaby and Camila screamed with excitement, pulling the boys up and out of their seats. "*Oh, oh, oh …*" They sang and sensually danced with the brothers.

Time flies by when you're having fun. Soon, Camila's mom spoiled the fun with a phone call.

"I'll be home soon. Going to buy some things with Gaby. Yes, Mother, bye," Camila said with annoyance. "Come on, my beloved," she said to Thiago, leading him down the hall and up the stairs by the hand.

Paulo threw Gabriela over his shoulder. "Whatever, Romeo and Juliet," he said, rushing past them and up the stairs, and Gaby muttered something about him not dropping her on her head as he continued to run.

Kids think they know everything, and these four were no exceptions. Good thing they were responsible and had protection, primarily thanks to Camila's mother instilling the fear of God in them.

They kissed, giggled, laughed, and the beers helped calm jittery nerves and uncertainty. "I love you," Thiago said to Camila as he helped her undress.

"I love you too," she said, passionately kissing him.

Their special moment was magical. Thiago had been waiting for this day for so long. Camila was the love of his life, and this was something he would cherish forever.

For Camila, it had to be Thiago because he was the sweetest person she knew, and she knew, without any doubt, that she would love him for the rest of her life.

However, they fell asleep once "the deed" was done … which was a big mistake for my friends.

EPISODE TWO

Camila's mother had called the police when she could not reach her daughter. Fortunately, they advised her to wait until morning, that she was probably at the boyfriend's house, and we can all guess what happened next, right? Yup! She went over to Thiago and Paulo's house.

The doorbell rang, startling Gaby. *Shit! What time is it? Ouch, my coochie hurts*, she thought.

Mine too! she heard Camila say in her head and jumped out of Paulo's bed in shock.

"What the fuck?" She looked around the room but only saw Paulo still sleeping, and before she could have another thought, Camila was barging into the room. They stared at each other curiously.

"Why were you in my head?" Camila asked Gaby, standing at the door.

"Why were you in mine?" Gaby shot back.

"Anyway …" Camila said, going into the room and shutting the door.

"Nice tits, now get dressed. Mama Bear is downstairs making a scene, and the last thing I want is for her to catch me here. We can discuss everything else later. So we're sneaking out the back door. Losing our virginity is already too much for one day," Camila continued tensely.

Gaby's face was ashen as she hurried to the bed. "Wake up, Sleeping Beauty," she said, shaking Paulo's shoulder.

"What?" Paulo asked, waking up.

"Mama Bear is here. We need to sneak out before she sets the house on fire with us in it," Gaby said, and Paulo looked at her, alarmed.

"That's bad, that's *very* bad!" he said, getting out of bed, looking for his underwear on the floor, and noticing Camila was in the room.

"You mind?" he said to Camila, who was biting her nails.

"Oh, please, just hurry the hell up!" she snapped.

Camila was a nervous wreck. She wasn't sure what her mother was capable of and didn't want to find out.

Mrs. De Los Santos didn't dislike the boys, but she was not fond of them either. I know. I'm trying to wrap my head around that too. I guess she doesn't like the idea that Camila has a boyfriend. Maybe she's hoping she will join a nunnery or something.

"Mrs. De Los Santos, for the last time, they're not here. They stopped by earlier and left. Please go home and wait for her there. I'm sure they'll turn up soon. Some girls from school were having a sleepover to discuss prom dresses. Camila probably didn't tell you because you don't let her go anywhere," Thiago told Camila's mother, his heart beating out of his chest.

Paulo escorted the girls out the back door as Thiago lied to Camila's mother through his teeth. I can't blame him. He was scared shitless of Camila's mother. They all were.

The girls rushed home, arm in arm. There was a cool breeze, and the moon was full, gloriously shining as if smiling triumphantly upon them. They burst out in nervous laughter as soon as they turned the corner.

"That was fun," Gaby said lightly, shoving Camila, and they giggled the rest of the way.

"I can't wait to have more adventures with you, Gaby," Camila said once they were in front of their houses.

"Thanks for being the realest," Camila told her, and Gaby hugged her tightly.

"I love you too, my sweet cornball," Gaby said, and they rushed into their houses, hearts still racing.

It was drizzling as Gabriela walked across the driveway to Camila's house the following day.

"Good morning, tia.[16] Is Camila around?" Gaby asked Camila's mother, afraid to make eye contact.

Camila's mom doesn't know how to let stuff go. She will bring mischief up from third grade, and Gaby hoped she didn't ask her any questions or reprimand her.

"Yes, she's in her room," she said, looking Gaby up and down, rolling her eyes, mumbling in Spanish. Gaby ran in before Mrs. De Los Santos could breathe fire and incinerate her where she stood.

It smelled like Fabuloso. She must have been cleaning since the crack of dawn. She had a beautiful home but overfurnished if you ask me. There is not a corner she doesn't have a vase, a table, or some decorative art piece, but she has good, expensive taste.

"Knock, knock …" Gaby said, opening the door without actually knocking on it, and Camila looked up, ready for combat.

"Oh, it's you!" Camila said, relieved. "Mom's been driving me crazy all day, saying the same thing repeatedly, like I'm two years old. I'm moving out as soon as I turn eighteen and graduate," Camila told Gaby, still upset.

Gaby laughed. "Stop being a drama queen. Just yes her to death, tell her what she wants to hear, and do whatever you want. That's what I do," Gaby said with a wink.

Gaby brushed her teeth and ran over, still in her pajamas. She was anxious to talk to Camila about what had happened last night.

Camila gave Gaby the middle finger. "Your mom isn't nearly as annoying as mine. Plus, I need peace. She's nonstop with the speeches and sermons!" Camila whined, pressing the pillow over her face and screaming into it.

Gaby jumped on Camila's bed, landing on her side, head resting on her palm. Camila's bedroom set was brown. The wood looked sturdy and antique, with matching nightstands and a large vanity. Her mother preferred furniture that looked traditional to the more modern styles.

"Enough with Mama Bear. Tell me about last night," Gaby said, resting her head on the fluffy pillow and staring at the ceiling. Camila still has the glow-in-the-dark stickers from when she was little up there.

---

[16] Aunt

Camila loved candles. She was burning one that smelled like cinnamon, and Gaby took a deep breath, inhaling the sweet aroma.

Gaby wished it was a sunny day as she noticed how gloomy Camila's room felt with the curtains still drawn and poor lighting.

Camila hadn't left her room and was still in pajamas too.

"I'm not telling you shit, you creep," Camila told her jokingly.

"Whatever, ho," Gaby said, laughing. "I have to say, it wasn't what I expected. It was painful," she admitted seriously now.

Camila rested her head next to Gaby's and stared at the stars on her ceiling, thinking she should have them removed. She's a woman now and ready to rid herself of childish things.

"I know what you mean, but it was everything I expected and more for me," Camila said.

Gaby rolled her eyes. "Here we go. Romeo, Romeo, where art thou, Romeo?" she said mockingly with her hands across her chest.

Like the Ibeyi, these two are very different. Camila is a romantic like Thiago, but Gaby is not.

"Whatever," Camila said. "I'm more interested in knowing why I heard you in my head," she said, looking at Gaby questionably.

"Why are you looking at *me* like that? How am *I* supposed to know?" Gaby asked defensively.

That whole hearing of Camila's thoughts was also a mystery to her. It's a mystery to me. How can this be possible?

Monday was a half day of school, and Gaby persuaded Camila that it would be a waste of time showing up, so they skipped school, and guess where they went instead? You got it. To see yours truly.

The boys were worried, hoping the girls didn't get in trouble … or worse, that they had been disappointed and didn't want to see them again.

"What if they switched schools?" Thiago asked Paulo that morning.

"Bro, stop. They're fine. Maybe they're not feeling well or didn't want to come on a half day," Paulo told him.

The girls didn't speak to them much the rest of the weekend, preoccupied with figuring out their telepathy, and of course, that didn't sit well with the boys, especially after what happened.

"It's a school day during school hours. Why are you ladies here?" I asked, scolding them. I didn't want any problems with Camila's mother either.

"Idely," began Camila. That's what they call me. They address everyone appropriately, but they call me Idely. When I asked them about it once, all I got was some lame excuse from Gaby.

"It's a compliment, and you look thirty, not forty-five. You're a hot lady with that flawless chocolate skin and caramel eyes. Plus, you have a banging body. Just look at that ass! It would sound weird calling you Ms. Perez," Gaby said, smoothing it out.

She also asked, "What kind of name is Idelfonsa?"

I told her it was a family name. My mama's name was Idelfonsa, and my grandmother's too. So Idelfonsa was the name given to the first female born into slavery in our family in Cuba. So we have passed it down through the generations.

"Something weird happened to us," Camila went on. "I heard Gaby's thoughts in my head, and she heard mine in hers. Can you tell us anything about why that would happen?" Of course, she asked like *I* have the answer to everything. I usually do, but still …

I've been reading many new-age books over the last couple of years, staying up to date and ordering useful, interesting merchandise for my business.

You must give the customers what they want. So I've been selling more crystals and chakra paraphernalia to keep up with demands, even books. Well, you get it.

But back to this most exciting occurrence. From what I've read on energy, I speculate that no two people are vibrating at the same frequency, so they experience reality from their unique energetic resonance, like a radio.

Everyone has their specific station. Yet, Gaby and Camila have miraculously found a way to resonate at the same vibrational frequency because they somehow share the same channel.

I try to summarize it so that they can understand. "I think you two are vibrating on the same frequency." They look at me bewildered.

"What does that mean?" Camila asked.

"It means you can hear each other's thoughts," I laughed. So why do they think I know everything?

"*Yo soy bruja,*[17] not Albert Einstein," I told them, and we all laughed.

I had a customer, so I sent them to the storage room to organize it. It was messy back there, and I could use a hand, and since they wanted to be high school dropouts, I figured I might as well put them to work.

Once the customer left, I checked up on them and found them sitting on the floor with cell phones in hand.

As Gaby would say, they're "twinning" in matching outfits. Both wore black sweatpants with white T-shirts. Gaby's shirt had a picture of Camila on the front, and on the back, it read, "*Best Friend.*"

Camila's shirt had Gaby's face and said the same on the back. The shirts were a Christmas gift from Thiago.

"Working real hard, I see," I said, and they just shrugged their shoulders.

"We completed our task. But of course, we didn't have much to do since you're so organized," Gaby said, winking at me.

"Oh, please, don't sweet-talk me, lazy brat," I told her.

Gaby smiled, showing plenty of teeth.

"Come out here, Thelma and Louise. I'm not through with you," I told them, and they followed me out.

"So, tell me more about this telepathy," I said.

They shrugged their shoulders at the same time again. These two are more in sync than The Rockettes.

"It hasn't happened again," Camila informed me.

"We tried all weekend!" Gaby added with disappointment.

They sure did ... and neglected the boyfriends that deflowered them in the process. Excuse me while I laugh. I crack myself up sometimes.

"Tell me, what were the conditions when it happened?" I asked them.

"Well ..." Camila said apprehensively, "we were at Thiago and Paulo's place, and ..."

"Fast-forward, please!" I interrupted.

---

[17] I'm a witch.

"Right!" Camila said, embarrassed.

"Um, my mom showed up at their house making a scene. I was panicky when the doorbell rang. I had a bad feeling. Thiago went down to answer the door. When I heard Gaby say, 'Shit, my privates hurt,' I thought to myself instinctively, mine too, so I ran over to see what that was about and heard my mother yelling downstairs. I freaked out, so getting out of there became my priority. We didn't have time to discuss the telepathy," Camila told me.

"We tried all weekend to talk to each other in our heads, but nothing happened. We were on the internet reading about telepathy but found nothing that could explain what happened to us," Camila added, frustrated.

I looked from one to the other, at a loss for words.

"Stress!" I shouted after a few minutes of silence.

The girls looked at me like I had two heads but didn't say anything. I suspected they wanted me to elaborate, so I continued.

"Maybe it only happens when you're under stress or fear. I wonder if you can learn to harness that ability?" I asked rhetorically and walked away to my bookshelves, hoping to find a book on telepathy, but to my disappointment, there were none.

I sell all sorts of books, from how to read tarot cards to channeling for dummies.

"Well, it seems to me that you've just recounted that you were scared when you heard the doorbell because you instinctively knew it was your mother, and Gaby was startled. So perhaps strong emotions trigger it," I said, attempting to give them some sort of explanation.

"Yes, you could be right. I was scared shitless when I woke up and realized I was still at Thiago's!" Camila said.

"I won't ask how it went, but why don't you two go wait for the boys at their place and explain to them what happened to you? I'm sure they're stressed out because you two have been avoiding them after what was supposed to be a special night," I suggested.

"Oh my God, you're right! They probably think they suck!" Gaby said, laughing. She doesn't take anything seriously. I admired that about her.

"It was magical, by the way!" Camila said swooningly, eyes glittering and smile bright.

"OK, Juliet, don't tell me. Go tell Romeo before he drinks poison!" I suggested, and suddenly, she looked alarmed.

"Let's go!" Camila said to Gaby as she pulled her toward the exit. I watched in amusement. I must admit, my life is way more fun with them in it.

The girls got to the boys' house and told their mother they only had one class that morning and would wait for them to get home from school. Mrs. Silva offered them something to eat while they waited, and they accepted it with pleasure.

I guess I can do some research on the internet. I was reading whatever I could that night. There were cases of people who alleged to possess telepathic and telekinetic abilities, but it was hard to say. The internet is full of scammers and people in desperate need of attention.

Many offered courses on how to develop your psychic abilities, but let me tell you, I believe no one is out there better suited to help them than me. I don't want them to be lab rats in some freaky scientific experiment.

The next day, I had an idea and called the boys. I told them I needed their help, but they couldn't tell the girls. So they came to the botanica to see me after school. They told the girls they had to meet with their soccer coach and would see them later.

"I'm going to tell them the two of you were arrested and taken into police custody. Let's see if that triggers a fear or stress response from them," I said as soon as they arrived.

I know what you're thinking. My idea sounded like a science experiment, but hear me out. I have Gaby and Camila's best interests at heart.

Thiago and Paulo looked skeptical but agreed, if only to torture them or see how much they care. I don't know which one it was, but I was just glad they did.

"Okay," I said, "I'll text them separately, and we'll see what happens."

I texted Camila first. With her being the hopeless romantic, I hoped she would have the most dramatic reaction, and then I texted Ms. Nonchalant, Gaby. That girl takes nothing seriously.

Within minutes, the girls were texting Thiago, Paulo, and me back. "Don't answer. Remember you're in jail," I instructed them.

Thiago looked anxious. "I hope Camila doesn't call my mom," he said.

Shit! I didn't think of that in my haste. But knowing Camila, she probably will.

Camila read the text I sent her. "Thiago and Paulo got locked up!" She reread it a second time, ensuring she understood correctly.

"What! Why?" she replied. I didn't answer.

This can't be fucking happening. What the hell happened with those two? Thiago would never do anything criminal. So, if they're in trouble, it was probably Paulo's fault, Camila thought, pacing back and forth in her room, biting her nails.

The fuck it is! she heard Gaby yelling in her head, and she was furious.

Paulo is a troublemaker who knows what he did and dragged Thiago along with him, thought Camila looking up at the ceiling as if it were Gaby's face.

Shut up, Miss Goody Two-shoes. You and Thiago are not perfect, so stop blaming Paulo. Thiago is a grown, sex-having man! Gaby thought, and Camila rolled her eyes.

Camila was agitated, fearing that if Mama Bear found out, she would never be able to see Thiago again openly.

Whatever. Let's figure out what the hell happened. If my mom finds out, she will never let me hang out with them again, thought Camila as she put on her sneakers and ran downstairs.

"Going next door to Gaby's," she shouted as she hurried out the front door.

Gaby was already waiting with her front door opened. "Let's go see Idely," she said before Camila could get up the front steps.

Camila stopped. "Okay, come on. Let's go. Why are you still standing there?" she said, waving her hands in front of her.

Gaby giggled. "She said they're in jail, not that they died!"

"Shush," Camila rebuked her with an alarmed look across her face and a finger over her lips. "Someone could hear you, and why is everything a joke to you?" she says reprovingly.

Gaby shook her head. "I'll be back!" she shouted as she shut the front door. "Camila, you need to relax. Everything is not that serious. Maybe Thiago forgot his wallet or something," Gaby said, relaxed. She doesn't like to stress herself out, but Camila gets worked up about anything.

The bell on the botanica door alerted me that someone had entered. I looked over Thiago's shoulder, leaning on the counter in front of me.

"Here they come," I whispered to the boys when I saw it was the girls. They turned to see Camila and Gaby walking toward them.

"She looks good," Thiago whispered as he watched Camila approach.

Camila wore tight overalls with a long-sleeved crop top and hot-pink lipstick.

"What's going on?" Camila asked, indignantly shoving Thiago's arm as she reached him. "Why were you arrested?" she demanded.

He hugged her. "Aw, my baby loves me!" he murmured in her ear. She looked at him through squinted eyes.

"You haven't answered my question!" she said reproachfully.

"We didn't get arrested!" Paulo exclaimed, throwing up his hands, already tired of this pretense.

"It was a ruse," I said. "It was my idea," I confessed. Camila and Gaby looked at me, surprised.

"You are bad, Idelfonsa. Look at you. Pranking us. I like it!" Gaby said, smiling.

"You should've seen the look on this one's face," she said, pointing a Camila. "She had a panic attack, mostly troubled about Mama Bear finding out," Gaby informed us, and we all laughed ... except for Camila.

"I'm glad you guys find this funny," Camila said, still upset. "Why would you do something like that, Idelfonsa? It was very immature of you."

This girl needed to ease up a little. She is not eighteen yet and acts like she's thirty-five already. The others are all eighteen and don't have the maturity she does.

"Because I wanted to test a theory," I told her.

"Since when did you become a scientist?" Camila asked me, folding her arms across her chest.

"Ever since the two of you became telepathic," I replied, rolling my eyes and neck. Is she for real?

They come to me with this situation, and now Camila dares to sass me. I only wanted to help them figure this out, and I know that's why they came to me in the first place. Spirituality begins where science ends.

Camila and Gaby were the literal personifications of soul sisters. Fate has brought them together, and maybe this is why. They are bound to each other.

We often think of soul mates as romantic partners, but a soul mate can be someone we have a soul contract with, despite the relationship.

"You want to hear my theory or not?" I asked, and they all stared at me.

"Yes!" the girls responded. And, of course, you already know how: simultaneously!

"Well, I believe you're both tuned into the same frequency." They looked at me like I was crazy. "Like the same radio station," I continued, ignoring the looks.

"Fear and stress triggered your telepathy, but maybe if you quiet your mind and try to reach the other mentally, you can do it at will. Maybe, if you practice before sleep at night, you'll get better results when you are more relaxed," I said with little conviction, but what the hell do I know about this?

Camila looked at me doubtfully. "How exactly do you suggest we do that?" she asked sarcastically.

"Instead of using a phone, just call each other in your mind until you get a response. Then reach out with your thoughts. You have a connection. You simply need to learn how to dial in," I answered. Hopefully, they understand.

Gabriela laughed. "You know you can speak out loud, right?" she asked Camila and me. "That night at Thiago and Paulo's house, I had the thought, but when you accused Paulo of getting them in trouble, I said what I was thinking out loud," she finished.

Paulo looked hurt. "Wait, you thought it was *my* fault we got arrested?" he asked Camila.

"Not now!" Camila barked at him and turned to Gaby.

"You know words are spoken thoughts, right?" Camila enlightened Gabriela. A lightbulb went off in Gaby's head, and they laughed.

I smiled as they left and waved goodbye. I can't wait to see what happens next.

EPISODE THREE

"What now?" Thiago asked Camila on the car ride home.

"Do you think you guys will be able to control it? It would be an awesome superpower to have during the state tests. You both can help each other out!" he suggested.

He shouldn't give Gaby any ideas on using their newfound abilities for illicit gain; she teeters between good and bad ideas all the time, as it is.

Gaby reached over and ruffled his hair. "You're a freaking genius, Thiago!" she said.

Now, he's talking *her* language. Gaby may not be the most applied student, but she has the kind of intelligence books can't buy.

"I don't know," Camila said, preoccupied. "I'm afraid once this channel opens and she figures it out, I won't be able to keep this maniac out of my head," she said and looked back at Gaby, sticking out her tongue.

"I can't wait to be in that corny head of yours! It's probably all about Thiago in there," Gaby replied, and Camila just laughed. Thiago squeezed Camila's hand.

"I'm willing to pay for information," he told Gaby.

"We're in business!" she responded quickly.

"What happened to hoes before bros?" Camila asked Gaby.

"I don't know what you're talking about," Gaby replied. "I'll give you fifty percent. After all, they're your thoughts," she told Camila as she shoved her head.

"Hey, Camila, we can come to our agreement," Paulo said, poking Gaby on the side, and Gaby's eyes widened.

"Shit! Never mind, Thiago, there are many more interesting things in my head than Camila's," she said, laughing.

"Oh? Like what?" Paulo asked, and Camila and Thiago laughed as the others jokingly bickered in the backseat.

The boys dropped them off at the corner. Thiago had been avoiding Camila's mom after the incident in his house, and Mama Bear usually waits for Camila outside.

"Hey," Camila said to Gaby as she went into her house, "I'll try to call you tonight. So listen out for me."

Gaby smiled. "Always, sweet cakes," she said, blowing her a kiss, and they both entered their houses and locked the doors.

That night, Camila was in bed thinking of Gaby. *Can you hear me?* she thought. *Are you there?* Camila beckoned, but nothing happened. She could not hear Gaby. *Maybe Idelfonsa is wrong*, she thought. *Maybe we can't control it. Maybe it was a freak occurrence*, Camila reasoned as she fell asleep. *I could be wrong, but I doubt it.*

In her bedroom, Gaby was doing the same. *Hey, cornball, can you hear me?* she continued through the night unsuccessfully.

I'm confident that they'll figure this out. If anyone can do it, it's Camila and Gabriela. I expect great things from them, and so should you.

My body ached, and my screams reverberated throughout my entire body. The sun was beaming hot, and the sweat burned my eyes. Another whip forcibly landed across my back, and I could feel the skin rip open and fresh blood flowing. Again, the pain was unbearable; my face was on the ground, dirt in my mouth, another whip, this time with extra vigor, and the end of it caught the side of my face. I passed out.

Camila had another dream and woke up crying. I feel these aren't dreams but memories of a past life or ancestral experience, but only time will tell. The girls have been trying to call each other every night for the past couple of weeks. They have had some success, but it's sporadic.

I tell them to keep at it and not to give up. It could be significant, and I'm sure it is no coincidence that Camila and Gaby have this ability. Regrettably, the exams have passed, and they didn't cheat as they wanted. Fortunately, they passed with flying colors, like I knew they would.

Many things are coming up for them, like the prom, Camila's birthday, and graduation. Today, they're in my shop. I don't remember if I mentioned it, but they come often.

"Idley, look!" Gaby said, taking out her prom dress. It's a beautiful off-the-shoulder, curve-hugging red dress. She will look magnificent in it, with her incredible figure and bleached curls.

"It's fitting for a queen, my love; absolutely gorgeous," I told her. She held it up against her body and twirled around the shop, imagining she was dancing in it.

"I told her red was a good choice. She looked stunning when she tried it on in the store," Camila said with a smile as we watched Gaby dance around with the dress like she was somewhere else.

"Where's yours?" I asked Camila, and she took it out.

She showed me an equally lovely lavender halter-strap princess gown. She too had a spectacular body. "You will look like royalty, my young goddesses," I said to them affectionately.

I can't wait for prom! Camila thought with excitement as she got ready for bed.

I can't wait for the hotel, motel, Holiday Inn after party. She heard Gaby sing in her head, and they both laughed. They were getting better at telepathically communicating, and the sex was getting better too. As you can see, normal, freaky teenagers.

"What's so funny?" Camila's mother asked, coming into her room without knocking. She's so strict that she probably stands outside Camila's door listening to her conversations.

"Do you mind? At least knock, lady," Camila told her, exasperated.

"This is *my* house. I don't *need* to knock, laughing alone. *Éstas en la edad del pavo todavía,*"[18] she said, leaving her room.

So annoying! Camila thought as her mother left.

Let me guess. Mama Bear! Gaby said through laughter.

You know it! Camila replied, still agitated, and heard Gaby still laughing in her head.

I asked my parents for a trip as a graduation gift. You want to come with me? Gaby asked Camila as if she would go anywhere without her. After all, they're attached at the hip and do most things together.

Where to? Camila inquired.

I was thinking Cuba, Gaby said, knowing Camila had mentioned it was on her bucket list, and she wanted to pick a place that Camila would find exciting.

I don't think we can travel there, Camila responded with disappointment.

I read somewhere we can enter from another country, like Canada or Mexico. Then we can ask Idely to come with us! Gaby said enthusiastically.

There was silence for a while, but Gaby felt a pleasant sensation of being at the beach. Maybe Camila thought about that, and she felt the feeling, although she couldn't see what Camila was seeing.

OK, we can ask Idely tomorrow. Good night, Camila said after a while of fantasizing.

In her imagination, Camila was in Cuba with Thiago. But, of course, the other two were there. They're on beach chairs, sunbathing, listening to the waves crashing on the shore, music playing, laughter, and drinks in hand—the whole nine yards.

"Good night," Gaby said, feeling the sun's warmth and drifting off to sleep.

It was Saturday. I had just opened. "Idely, Idley," I heard my name being sung and turned to see my two favorite girls, Camila and Gaby.

"It's too early. Shouldn't you be preparing for prom? So, why are you here?" I asked them.

---

[18]   You're still in the awkward stage.

They held hands like little girls, giggling and jumping up and down. "You two win the lotto or something? You're way too happy," I said, a little nervous.

They laughed. "No, not lotto. We brought our dresses. You said you know how to fix them if we needed it," Gaby answered.

"We also want to go on a trip after graduation!" they said in harmony. They always say the same thing at the same damn time. It's so weird!

"Oh yeah? And where are you big spenders going?"

"Cuba!" they said. Do I even need to tell you how? I didn't think so.

Gaby shook me by the shoulders. "But we need you, Idely," she said, and I looked at her inquisitively.

"What for?" I asked, afraid of the answer.

"Because your family was from Cuba. We plan on traveling to Canada and then to Cuba from there," Gaby rambled.

They know good and well that they can't travel directly to Cuba. So, instead, they are doing some shady way around it, undoubtedly creating a mess, and are trying to drag me along.

"No, thank you! Not interested," I answered firmly.

"Why?" Camila asked, whining.

I thought Camila would speak some sense into the crazy one, but Gaby was becoming more influential, I see.

"Because we can get fined! I'm not wasting my life's savings paying a fine to visit Cuba. I know I will go, but not now—not like that," I said, harried.

They puckered their lips and gave me the sad puppy face, holding hands with interlocked fingers.

"Please, please, we want to go to Cuba!" they exclaimed, then vanished. They were erased right before my eyes. They no longer stood before me as if they ceased to exist. They just disappeared into thin air. It happened fast, like the twinkling of an eye—imperceptible. Except they were standing right in front of me.

One second, they were there, and the next, they were gone.

"*Eleguá no juegues conmigo*,"[19] I said clutching my *elekes*.[20] I closed my eyes. Maybe I was hallucinating; they were never here, and I was utterly insane.

"Idelfonsa …!" I heard my name screamed and opened one eye. They had instantly materialized in front of me again.

I was stunned as I opened my other eye, and so were they. I have seen many weird, strange, unusual, and seemingly miraculous things before, including their telepathy, but this was a whole 'nother level. We examined each other for a long moment without speaking.

Quietly, I walked to the door, turned the sign *open* to *closed*, and locked it. The girls were still hugging each other, visibly shaken.

"Come on," I said, holding their joined elbows and walking them up to the house.

It took a while to climb the stairs because their knees were shaking, and they looked terrified. Even I was shaken. This was something out of a movie, and I felt ill-equipped to handle such a situation for the first time. So I silently invoked my Orisha[21] to help us.

"You want some water?" I asked as they sat on my white leather sofa.

They nodded, still unable to speak. I brought the girls water, and they sipped it slowly. I sat beside them, and we were silent for a while.

I would like the initial shock to subside before I ask any questions. They needed to register what had happened first. This incident was traumatic.

As would be expected, Gabriela was over it first. "Oh my fucking God!" she said, her eyes wild. "You are not going to believe it," she continued.

"Try me," I replied. I mean, I was there. I witnessed the whole thing. So if someone was going to believe it, it had to be me because you had to see it to believe it—and I did.

"We went somewhere else!" Gaby exclaimed.

No shit, Sherlock, I thought to myself, nodding my head. I hoped Camila snapped out of it quickly.

---

19   Eleguá (Yoruba/Ifa/Lucumí/Santeria deity) Don't play with me.
20   Beads
21   Emissaries of Olodumare or God Almighty, often referred to as guardian angels.

"I think it was Cuba," Camila said to my relief.

I suspected that much as we sat there. Then finally, I concluded that since Camila and Gaby were telekinetic, and Cuba was where they had wished to go, that's where they went.

"It happened quickly, but I think we were in a *Malecon*.[22] I thought I saw the Cuban flag waving as we teleported back. We freaked out. All we could think about was getting back here to you," Camila said, her eyes blank.

Now, that's something new. They can also teleport! It's as if we're on the *Enterprise*, and I am Captain freaking Kirk. So what's next? They can fly?

"Can we get ready here?" Camila asked me.

As if it couldn't get any worse because you know what that means, right? Yes, *I* have to call Mama Bear.

"Sure," I replied, struggling to sound sympathetic.

What was I going to tell Camila's mother? I know all about her, but I doubt she knows anything about me. However, I'm sure I'll think of something, right?

Politely and charmingly, I introduced myself. "Good morning. My name is Idelfonsa."

"*Quien?*"[23] Camila's mother asked, bothered. I bet she'll pretend not to speak English if I become a telemarketer.

I considered going with the prank to see if she would, but I had already given my name. Shit, I should've thought of that before.

"I am a friend of Camila and Gabriela. I own the botanica near Yonkers High School, where they attend," I said, pausing.

"*Cristo reprende!*"[24] she whispered, and I could picture her making the sign of the cross. I covered the phone and laughed.

"What happened? Are they OK?" she asked, concerned.

"Yes, they're fine. I'm doing alterations on their gowns, which might take a few hours since I have to do it between customers." I lied because I didn't want to deal with it.

---

[22] Stone-built embankment or esplanade along a waterfront.
[23] Who?
[24] Christ rebuke!

"OK, *ya son grande*!"[25] she said after an awkward silence.

"You owe me!" I said to Camila, and she gave me a forced smile.

"What do you think happened to us, Idely?" Gaby asked.

Like I said before, they think I know everything. "Who do I look like to you? Nikola Tesla?" I asked, pacing back and forth, trying to think of something.

"The two of you are not only telepathic but telekinetic, and that is somehow enabling you to teleport," I stated.

"Gaby, quick—think of being in your bedroom right now! Really desire it," I suggested. She stared at me blankly for a few seconds, then closed her eyes. Nothing happened.

"It's not working," she said after a few minutes of trying.

"I think you both have to do it for it to work," I said, and they gazed at each other. I was sure that the girls were telepathically communicating.

"Not working," Camila said after a few minutes, and I scratched my head.

They were giving me sad faces and holding hands right before they disappeared.

"I got it! You need to touch and hold hands. It's probably a combination of your energy that produces the effect." Camila looked nervous. "Go ahead," I encouraged. "Try it!" I pushed, and Camila quietly shook her head.

"Oh, come on, scaredy-cat. Let's see what we can do!" Gaby insisted, extending her hand, and Camila, disquieted, took it.

"Think of Gaby's—" Before I could finish, they were gone.

In case you're wondering, it wasn't like in the movies, with flashing lights, wind, and a big production. Instead, it was quiet and quick, almost like they were collapsing into themselves.

I'm not sure of its science, or if there is any, but I know my girls are extraordinary. The first time I saw them, I knew they were special.

I went down to the botanica to tell my brother, Lazaro, I had locked the door, but he had already figured it out. He was escorting a customer to the exit.

---

[25] They're adults now.

I know! I haven't mentioned Lazaro before, but I thought it was inconsequential. Of course, the girls were the primary focus, but I suppose now that I will be playing a significant role in this epic adventure, he's worth mentioning.

My brother and I own this business. He does consult with clients. He's a *Babalawo*,[26] so he is always busy.

"*Acere, que bola contigo?*"[27] he asked as he walked back into the consulting room, cigar smoke filling the air.

He probably already knows something strange and unusual is going on. He stopped and looked in my eyes. "*Preparate pa' lo viene con esas muchachas!*"[28] he said, shutting the door behind him.

That was ominous, I thought to myself.

Camila and Gaby stood in Gaby's room, looking at it as if for the first time. The neatly drawn, opened gray and white striped curtains allowed sunlight to flood the room. Her bedroom set was modern, with beautiful white wood, and the bed's headboard had sparkling crystal tufting, which gave it an elegant look.

The skillfully made bed with a gray plush comforter gave the room a regal appearance, and a sweet vanilla scent permeated the air.

They sat on the bed. "This is so amazing, Cami," Gaby said.

Camila was silent, unsure how she felt about all of this. If she couldn't rationally explain it, it scared her.

"Imagine the places we could visit. The possibilities are endless," Gaby said earnestly.

Camila smiled but looked concerned. "Why is this happening to us?" she asked her friend.

Gabriela took her hand. "Because we are freaking awesome, and the Universe wants us to, *that's* why!" she said to Camila reassuringly.

That's the beautiful thing about these girls. They complement each other. Where one is uncertain, the other is sure. Camila overanalyzes everything, and Gaby just goes with the flow.

The perfect yin and yang bring balance and harmony.

"Don't worry so much. If we were not worthy of these gifts, we

---

[26] A priest of the highest order belonging to the Santeria religion.
[27] Mate, what are you up to?
[28] Prepare for what is to come with those girls.

wouldn't have them, so let's make the best of it!" Gaby assured her.

Camila nodded. Gaby was right. Nothing happens by chance, and there are no coincidences.

"Oh, now that I'm here, let me grab some things I'll need to get ready," Gaby said, walking to her dresser.

"Good thinking. We should go to my room next. I need to grab my shoes," Camila said, thinking of everything she needed.

Gaby packed a bag, and as soon as she finished, she went over and took Camila's hand.

"I want to go to Camila's room!" she said aloud, and Camila shook her head, foreseeing themselves getting caught because Gaby couldn't shut up.

Camila told her to be quiet. She doesn't want Mama Bear to catch them. It would be difficult to explain what they were doing in there since I had called and told her they were at my place.

Gaby adhered to the warning. She didn't want Mrs. De Los Santos to catch them. She felt her patience wearing thin.

Camila quickly gathered what she needed and took Gaby's hand as they smiled. Camila was getting comfortable with her new ability and maybe even a little happy about it. I wanted her to relax and embrace this with enthusiasm.

They're back at my place now, and I hear them calling my name. "I'm down here," I yelled, and they came running down.

"We think we've figured it out," Camila said confidently.

"Yeah, and good thing we did. I realized that all we had to get ready for prom were the gowns. So we grabbed everything we needed from our rooms," Gaby added.

I smiled. I was happy to see Camila embracing this gift of theirs.

It was time. Camila and Gaby were ready for prom and looked stunning. Thiago and Paulo's parents were at the Poconos for the weekend, and the girls planned to spend the night at their place.

Camila had no idea how she would pull off spending the night at Thiago's house before discovering her new abilities. Now that they could magically teleport themselves wherever they wanted, that wouldn't be a problem since she was more confident and willing to take advantage of her newfound powers.

The boys arrived looking dapper and handsome in their tailored suits. "You all look fantastic," I said, taking their photo.

They posed for a few more photographs, and then they were off.

"Have fun," I said as I waved them off, teary-eyed. I don't have children, so this is as close as it gets me.

The boys held the doors open as the girls climbed in, and I looked on with pride. Thiago and Paulo's parents did a great job raising them.

"Bye!" they said as they waved, and I watched the car until it disappeared out of sight.

The venue chosen was beautiful. Everyone looked fabulous as they filed into the hall. Some arrived in limos, excited parents dropped off some, and as you already know, my kids drive themselves.

The music was loud, and the room was dimly lit, with alternating color sequences. A traditional ice sculpture adorned a table.

Dusk cloaked the area as the sun set, and the sky was clear. It was warm, and the energy was electric. Everyone was happy and full of excitement.

Prom night will be the last night the students spend together as the Senior Class of 2012. Soon, people will be headed their separate ways, embarking on exciting new adventures, but for now, everyone enjoyed the moment and had the time of their lives.

They danced all night, and it felt like it was just them, for the most part. No one else mattered. They watched as the king and queen were crowned, then continued dancing. The girls and two brothers never really made other friends and stuck together since that first year.

"We're already a crowd!" Camila used to say. "We don't need to hang out with any more people."

They didn't start dating until the end of their sophomore year, so she wasn't wrong, and sophomore year, when a boy named David tried to get close to them because he had a crush on Camila, Thiago was convinced she was right.

I can't blame him, but he hadn't yet told her how he felt, and already he had to compete for her attention.

Gaby had dated a boy named Mike for like two weeks that year but broke up with him because, as she liked to put it, he was a lousy kisser.

I think she did it to make Paulo jealous, and she succeeded because before the school year ended, the boys professed their love, and they have been inseparable ever since.

EPISODE FOUR

Thiago and Paulo pulled into the driveway between Gabriela's and Camila's houses. Then they quickly exited the vehicle to open the doors for the girls. Usually, the girls will protest about being able to open their own doors, but not tonight.

I like to tell them that being respected and treated with high regard is not patriarchal but a demonstration of love. Disregarding certain customs because they are now frowned upon is ignorance.

"Think for yourselves," I tell them any chance I get. "Draw your own conclusions from your own experiences and not from what others tell you," I constantly say.

Mama Bear was peeking through the curtain as they said their goodbyes.

"See you soon," Camila whispered in Thiago's ear as she gently kissed his cheek.

"Hotel, motel, Holiday Inn …" Gaby sang as she winked at Paulo and headed for Camila's front door.

I didn't tell you the plan, but Gaby was spending the night at Camila's for all intents and purposes, if you know what I mean.

In good spirits, Mrs. De Los Santos opened the door before they reached it. It must be all the wine she consumed while she waited. Mama Bear means well. Camila wouldn't be an exceptional young lady if it weren't for her.

"Did you ladies have fun?" she asked the girls as they hurried into the house.

"Yes, tia, it was a good time!" Gaby replied with joy.

"*Y tú, mija?*"[29] she asked Camila with a smile.

"I had a great time, Ma," Camila said, hugging her, and her mother kissed her forehead.

"I'm exhausted," Gaby said as they walked up to Camila's room.

"Me too. I want to go right to sleep!" Camila exclaimed.

"Good night!" they said simultaneously with a ring of excitement in their voices.

Once they entered the room, Gaby said, "OK, let's go!"

Camila shook her head. "I know her. She's going poke her head in to see what we're up to with the pretext of a good night," Camila explained.

"So we're not going?" Gaby asked, disappointed.

"Of course, we're going. We need to change into some pj's and get in bed. Once Mom says good night, I'll ask her to shut the lights, and she'll be gone," Camila said.

"Cool. Are my pj's in the same drawer as usual?" Gaby asked, walking over to the dresser, and Camila nodded. They helped each other out of their gowns, changed into pajamas, and settled into bed.

Like clockwork, Camila's mother cracked the door open. "You ladies need anything before I go to sleep?" she asked happily.

"Yes, can you please shut the lights?" Camila asked, and she did.

"Good night. I love you, girls!" she said as she shut the door, and they replied in unison, "We love you too!" There is no fiercer love than that of a mama bear.

"You ready?" Camila asked Gaby, giddy with excitement.

"Let's get out of here!" Gaby exclaimed joyfully, taking her hand.

I'm also excited. I want the girls to embrace their gifts and make the best of this unique opportunity. It is not our inadequacies we often fear but our power.

The stirring is in all of us. The yearning for something more significant is always present, yet we do not follow it. We do not surrender to the calling, creating a void. This vortex sucks the life force from us, causing anxiety, depression, addiction, and anything detrimental to the human soul.

---

[29]   And you, my daughter?

There are many things I haven't revealed yet. So, bear with me. The boys will be moving, having been accepted to the Massachusetts Institute of Technology. Paulo will be studying computer science and Thiago mechanical engineering.

The girls will both attend NYU for liberal arts and sciences. I still don't know what that means, but I hope for the best. I hope they figure out what they want to do because this NYU business costs their parents a pretty penny.

On a serious note, they don't like to discuss that they will be apart from each other. The distance is a sore subject. Camila had a serious discussion about ending their romantic relationship and remaining friends once they start college in the fall, but Thiago refused, and they haven't discussed it since. Paulo and Gaby don't think that far ahead. They live in the moment.

Camila set the alarm for six in the morning. This girl lives decades ahead of her age, carefully considering everything. There would be hell to pay if her mother peeked in her room and didn't find them there. Camila will ensure she stays in her mom's good graces for as long as possible.

Wake up! she thought forcibly of Gaby, uncertain that it would work, but it did. So, it seems they have figured it out after all.

Oh my God! Seriously? she heard Gaby in her head.

Yes, come here. We have to go, Camila instructed, and Gaby rolled her eyes, leaning over to kiss Paulo.

"I have to go, sunshine," she said in his ear and tiptoed to Thiago's room.

Camila was on her feet. "Let's go!" Camila commanded, grabbing Gaby's hand.

"Always so uptight," Gaby said, thinking of Camila's room.

Once in her room, Camila sighed with relief.

"Relax. She was drinking her wine last night and in a good mood. So we're good," Gaby said, sensing Camila's tension.

"Oh, be quiet. I'm going back to sleep. I had a long night," Camila said, and Gaby tickled her.

"Little slut!" Gaby said, and Camila elbowed her.

"Yeah, and I suppose you were praying all night, right?" Camila asked, and they laughed and fell asleep again.

Graduation Day finally arrived. The kids invited me, and although I've known them since they started high school, I felt a little awkward attending. So I told them I couldn't but showed up anyway.

The auditorium was full of parents and caregivers beaming with pride, many with happy tears, knowing that the kids would be heading off to college at summer's end.

Camila's mother was sobbing. Her baby and only child was now grown-up. Now, she had to loosen her grip.

Tanisha Brown, the valedictorian, took the stage, and the auditorium erupted in applause and cheers. She delivered a beautiful and emotional speech.

"Remember, we are powerful beyond our wildest imagining, capable of greatness. So, let us go forth and achieve our highest potential!" she concluded, and the crowd erupted again, many with tears in their eyes and hope in their hearts.

They sang as they marched down the aisle, and I cried as I saw them with tears and smiles on their faces.

The song played on. By now, the auditorium was nearly empty, and I went outside to find them.

"Idelfonsa!" they cried, running in my direction. "You came!" Camila said happily.

I hugged her. "Honey, I wouldn't have missed it for the world. I'm proud of all of you!"

I congratulated them on their achievements. Then Camila and Gaby introduced me to their parents.

The girls said they'll be volunteering at the botanica over the summer as part of an assignment for a sociology class. I nodded, even though that's the first I heard of it.

What are these two up to and haven't told me? I nervously thought.

"How did I get so lucky?" I said sarcastically, and they both squeezed my hand.

My best friend, Carmen, will be visiting from Puerto Rico. It devastated me when she moved about ten years ago, but I'm glad she'll be with me for a few weeks. Maybe she can give me a hand with whatever these two are cooking up.

I often wonder what it would have been like if Carmen and I had those abilities. I can tell you this much. We would've taken the world by storm. Although this town was too small for the two of us as it is, we had a good time, and I'll leave it at that … with a wink.

The girls went out to eat after their graduation ceremony, and the boys and their families joined them. Gaby wore a short yellow dress, white sandals and had bright red lips.

Camila also wore a dress. Hers was white with black sandals and bright lips too. They looked beautiful. Thiago couldn't stop staring at Camila, and Mama Bear gave him dirty looks.

Soon after, Carmen arrived from Puerto Rico, and I was super excited.

"*Camai!*"[30] Carmen exclaimed as she came into the botanica and squeezed me so tight I couldn't breathe.

"*Acere*,[31] it's been too long," I said, kissing her cheek.

"*Ay bendito!*[32] I've missed you so much. I can't wait to meet the girls you've told me about."

We looked at each other in an embrace and hugged some more. It's good to see Carmen.

"*Ave Maria, qué calor!*"[33] Carmen said, putting down her suitcase.

"I'll get you a cold beer," I said as I closed the shop.

Lazaro came out of the consulting room, and the cigar smoke followed him, filling the air. "Looking good, woman," he told Carmen before we called it a night and went upstairs.

"You look great yourself, Lacho. I wonder if that syrup skin of yours is still sweet?" Carmen said lustingly.

"Come on, pervert," I said, pulling Carmen upstairs.

She and Lazaro had a brief fling when we were young. My mother swore Carmen would end up pregnant sophomore year. Lazaro was a senior then.

We drank beer, had dinner, and talked late into the night. I told her all about Camila, Gabriela, and my theories. She was fascinated and could not wrap her mind around it.

---

[30] Sister/girlfriend
[31] Mate
[32] OMG
[33] Hail Mary, it's hot

"*Chacho!*[34] That's unbelievable. I won't fully believe it until I see it," Carmen stated.

I knew what she meant. I wouldn't have believed it myself if I hadn't been standing there.

Carmen said she would help me with the botanica the following day, and I was grateful. I've been meaning to hire an extra hand. Then I heard the bell and turned to see who it was because we had just opened.

"Good morning, sunshine!" Gaby said with a radiant smile with Camila in tow, also smiling.

"Good morning, early birds," I said apprehensively.

"The early bird gets the worm," Camila said, winking.

Okay, I can't take this suspense anymore. I needed to know what these girls were up to now.

"What is it with you two, anyway?" I asked, looking at them carefully.

"We have a spectacular idea and know you'll *love* it!" Gaby said mischievously, and Camila nodded with excitement. The fact that Camila has so much enthusiasm was frightening.

"I can't wait to hear it," Carmen said, coming around to get a better look at them.

They were standing between aisles, and my back was toward the counter with the cash register, where Carmen was standing. I could feel her burning a hole in my back.

"I'm Carmen, by the way," she said to the girls.

"This is my best friend. She is visiting from Puerto Rico," I explained, seeing the strange looks they were giving her.

"When did you live in Puerto Rico?" Gaby asked me, completely disregarding Carmen.

"Nice to meet you. I'm Camila. She is Gabriela," Camila said politely.

"I've heard a lot about you ladies!" Carmen said, unbothered. "So, what's this great idea you have?" she asked them.

Full disclosure … Carmen is a lot like Gaby, a little reckless, if I'm honest. She got us in trouble plenty in school and at home.

---

[34] Oh boy!

Gaby beamed at her. "Well, we plan to travel the world this summer!" she exclaimed.

I looked at them, totally surprised. "You ladies have travel-the-world money?" I asked, fearing the answer. I hoped Gaby didn't convince Camila to teleport into bank vaults.

"Nope," Camila said. "We don't need money to go on a worldwide excursion." Carmen laughed.

"*Lo van a pagar con los pelos del cu—*"[35] Carmen said, and I interrupted her before she said anything vulgar. As I said, she's reckless.

"Ha, your friend is not only hot like you, Idely, but she's also funny," Gaby praised her.

Yes, my best friend is hot. Carmen has beautifully sun-kissed, tanned skin, green eyes, and bouncy, curly, blond hair, although she dyes it. But it suits her well.

"Idelfonsa!" Camila said thoughtfully. "We will teleport to different countries; we don't need money to do that," she told me.

Am I the *only* one having a bad feeling about this? I want them to embrace this, go back and forth between their bedrooms, and visit the boys at their dorms, but this travel-the-world business made me uncomfortable.

"Where will you sleep, on the street?" I asked them, and Gaby shook her head.

"No no no, you're getting this all wrong. We plan on visiting for the day. We leave early and return at nightfall. Easy peasy!" Gaby said triumphantly.

"That easy, huh?" I asked, still not sure this was a good idea.

I bet my botanica that Gaby came up with this, and Camila lost her mind by going along with it.

"I think it's a fantastic idea! I would do the same thing if I could teleport, but I'd make a pit stop at Fort Knox first," Carmen said with pleasure, and I looked at her, horrified.

"Please, don't give them any ideas," I said sternly.

"Just kidding, girls. Keep it legal and PG," she told them, winking.

---

[35] They will pay with the hair on their backside.

I was hoping she would help me keep this train on its track—not help derail it.

"PG left the station," I said, laughing.

"How does it work? Are you just going to crash-land in front of people? Wouldn't that cause alarm? I would be scared of getting detained or something … wouldn't you?" Carmen asked seriously now. She made a good point, one I had not considered before.

If they're going to do this, and I'm not saying I condone it, they need to plan every detail carefully.

"Carmen is right, girls. You need to think this through and plan carefully. You can't just pop in and out of places. It could be dangerous, and someone could record it," I said seriously.

"Yes, you're right!" Camila said. That girl has some sense because Miss Crazy will not think anything through logically.

"I also came up with the idea that we can record our adventures and upload them to YouTube," Camila said. Then just as I thought she had sense, she used the word "record," which blew me away. Now, I'm not sure what she's talking about.

"Where? And what?" I asked, confused.

"It's a channel on the internet where you can upload any content, and if you get a lot of views, you can get paid."

Is it me? Or is Camila starting to sound like Gaby now?

"We plan to make this business and pleasure," Gaby added.

I don't know. Now they want to have video evidence of their travels. That's the thing with this generation. They want to record everything.

"I love it!" Carmen shouted, and I rolled my eyes at her. "Where to first?" she asked, excited.

"Carmen, relax. Let's think this through and help them plan before they get themselves in trouble." Carmen smiled like a child, ran to the counter, and grabbed a pen and pad.

"Okay, let's plan, but first, I need to know where they're going. I know—Puerto Rico!" she cried out. "I live there. I can tell you a low transit place where you can land."

She looked at us uncertainly, and we laughed. "Do you? Land?" she asked innocently.

We didn't reply because we were too busy laughing. But, oh, I can't wait to see Carmen's face when these two disappear in front of her for the first time.

"Whatever!" She continued to be annoyed. "I can tell you where to go so you don't scare people to death."

"Sounds good!" Gaby said.

"I agree!" Camila exclaimed.

"I'd like to visit Old San Juan. Where can we best show up? And there's no landing. We just pop up on our feet at the next location. Flying would be cool, but not something we can do," Gaby told Carmen.

"Not yet, at least!" Camila chimed in eagerly.

I don't know if my heart can take any more superpowers. I don't watch many superhero movies, but I think that if they can teleport, they won't be able to fly. That doesn't seem fair, but with these two, who knows?

"I think a parking garage would best to avoid crowds. Doña Fela's parking garage will do. Then, you'll be right in the heart of Viejo San Juan," Carmen said enthusiastically.

"Oh my God, this is so exciting!" she continued before the girls could answer.

"Settle down, Wizard of Oz," I said because her encouragement was not helping.

"Are you sure you want to do this?" I asked the girls.

"Yes!" they exclaimed excitedly, "yes!" simultaneously!

"All right, you have my blessing then. Just be careful, have fun, and don't spend all your savings in one place. You have the rest of the world to see," I told them.

They held hands, waved at us, and disappeared.

Carmen stood frozen, blinking rapidly for a few minutes. I walked away and stood behind the counter, giving her time to recover. Finally, she turned around and jumped up with joy.

"*Esto está brutal!*"[36] she said, leaning on the counter with childlike glee. "Can you imagine if we could've been able to do that?" she asked, her eyes filled with wonder.

---

[36] This is awesome!

"Yeah, I can. But of course, we would still be in prison for break-ing into Fort Knox!" We laughed at the thought. Gaby is child's play, compared to Carmen in her day.

"What do we do now?" Carmen asked.

"We pray, and we wait," I said, holding my beads, hoping they'd have fun and not get into trouble or get recorded and blasted by media outlets.

As Carmen suggested, they arrived at the parking garage on the top floor. It was still early morning, and not many cars were there. Camila and Gabriel looked at each other, ecstatic.

"This is so cool!" Gaby said, still holding Camila's hand.

"I know!" Camila replied, smiling broadly.

They took the elevator to the street level and exited the park-ing garage. The sun shone brightly, the temperature was warmer than expected, and people happily walked around. The restaurant that I said was my favorite was right across the street, Raices.[37]

Every time I visited Carmen, we would walk around Old San Juan and eat at Raices. It didn't matter how many times I saw Old San Juan. I'm always fascinated by the richness of the culture and the kindness of the people on the island. I'm sure the girls will enjoy spending the day there.

Everything was bright and colorful, and the girls were mesmerized as they wandered the cobblestone streets of Old San Juan. They heard music and marveled at Gothic, Renaissance, and Baroque architecture. They spent the day seeing the Plaza de Armas, Casa Blanca, San José Church, San Cristóbal Castle, and El Morro.

They were so captivated by the beautiful and rich culture that they lost track of time and decided to eat before sunset.

The girls walked back to Raices, the restaurant I recommended, and sat outside to eat. They ordered Mofongo[38] and two piña coladas since Puerto Rico is the cocktail's birthplace.

"Happy Birthday, Camila!" Gaby said as they made a toast. "I hope you live a thousand years, and I get to see it!" With that salutation, they laughed.

---

[37] Roots
[38] A Puerto Rican dish with fried plantains as its main ingredient.

Sorry, with all the commotion, I forgot to mention it was Camila's eighteenth birthday, but don't worry. We have a cake waiting for her when she returns. Oh, and the legal drinking age in Puerto Rico is eighteen.

With their tummies full and happy hearts, they returned to the parking garage and took the elevator to the top floor. The sun had finally set, and Camila was anxious to get back.

She and Thiago had disagreed about spending her birthday without him, and her mother complained about her thinking she was grown, but for Camila, this was the perfect day, and it wasn't over.

She would make it up to Thiago upon return, but this had turned out to be more than she could've asked for, and she was incredibly grateful for her gift and for being able to share it with her best friend, Gabriela.

Camila and Gaby exited the elevator and headed to the end where there were no cars but stopped dead in their tracks. They heard arguing and sounds like punches and kicks striking a body. Afraid, they hid behind a vehicle to conceal themselves.

They watched as two men beat a third on the ground. "*Té voy a matar, cabrón*,"[39] they heard one tell the victim as they shoved him into a car's trunk.

As Camila looked on, Gaby was typing the vehicle's plate number on her phone. Then one of the assailants looked over to where they were hiding.

Camila let out a yelp, afraid they'd been seen, and pulled Gaby down. Suddenly, they heard footsteps coming in their direction.

Scared, Camila and Gabriela held hands as the footsteps came closer. The girls disappeared before the men reached the vehicle they were hiding behind.

---

[39] "I'm going to kill you." *Cabron* refers to someone who cheats.

EPISODE FIVE

"Oh my God!" they returned screaming. "Call the police, call the police!" They looked scared to death. Color had drained from their faces. They were pale, shaking, and still holding hands.

"What happened?" I asked wearily.

"We've just witnessed a kidnapping, possibly a murder!" Camila said, her eyes teary.

How can this be possible? I felt dizzy and sat down.

"I have the plate number; we must alert the police!" Gaby said.

"Call 911," Camila added.

I still couldn't process anything they were saying, but the word *murder* was ringing inside my head like a bell.

"No," Carmen told them.

"What?" Gaby asked, shocked.

"I mean, if we dial 911 here, we won't get the police in Puerto Rico, and explaining how you know this will be difficult," she explained.

She then picked up her phone and looked up something.

"I'll call the nearest police station in Puerto Rico and tell them what's going on," Carmen said and made the call, leaving an anonymous tip about a kidnapping that had just taken place.

She urged them to hurry because she feared the victim's life was in danger as Gaby showed her the phone so that she could relay the vehicle's plate number to them.

Camila paced back and forth. "What if they've already killed him? We didn't do anything!" she wailed.

I embraced her; she was still trembling, and her skin felt cold.

"You did what you could. You obtained a good description and a plate number. I believe that will make a difference. You ladies can teleport; you're not superheroes," I said, trying to calm her.

Gaby was sitting, but her leg was shaking violently as she loudly tapped her fingers on the counter.

"I'm going to make some tea," Carmen said, going upstairs. "We all need to relax. That was too much excitement and a big scare for one day." She climbed the stairs mumbling something about a heart attack in Spanish.

Thiago and Paulo showed up with Camila's birthday cake. "What happened?" Thiago asked as he saw the nervous expression on the girls.

"These two witnessed a crime on their way back," I said quickly.

"Are you OK?" Thiago asked as he placed the box containing the cake on the counter and rushed to Camila.

"I'm fine," she said, hugging him. "Better now that you're here," she said, and he kissed the top of her head and held her tightly against his body, softly caressing her hair.

"You good?" Paulo asked Gaby, ruffling her hair. She gave him a thumbs-up. "Good, let's have cake then!" he added.

I had put out balloons and a happy birthday banner, but I don't think Camila noticed.

Carmen came down with a pot of tea and some cups. "You got something a little stronger?" Gaby asked her, seeing the teapot with disappointment.

"No, she doesn't!" I said. "Now you want to underage drink in my place of business?!" I told her, appalled.

Gaby mimicked what I've just said and then stuck out her tongue. Real disrespectful.

"She goes on one trip, has a cocktail, and thinks that's what we do here. Unbelievable!" I muttered.

"You're closed for the day, and I just had a drink. So pretend we're in Puerto Rico," she said, seemingly calmer now that she was in a confrontation.

This girl lives for drama, I thought and smiled.

"How about you drink the damn tea and calm down?" I said, pouring some tea into a cup. Gaby screwed her mouth but took it.

Teenage girls have too much freaking attitude. I commend anyone who must deal with them permanently. Luckily for me, they go home.

Thiago took the cake out of the box, I lit the candles, and we sang happy birthday to Camila. Her spirits lifted immediately.

Then they told us about their wonderful time in Puerto Rico and all the fantastic sites they visited as we ate. Later, they calmly went over the abduction they witnessed.

"I wonder what happened. You think those assholes killed the guy?" Paulo asked, looking around at the rest of us.

"I hope not!" Camila said with horror.

"Hey, Carmen, you think you can call back and ask for an update?" Gaby asked.

Carmen nodded and stood up to make the call. She walked to the back of the shop, where all the statues of saints were, and we continued to talk amongst ourselves. I gave the kids more cake, and then Carmen returned.

"By the way, you look gorgeous, baby," Thiago said to Camila, who wore a long, tight, leopard print cami dress.

"Thank you, my love. You're hot," she said to him.

"They located the vehicle using the description and plate number you ladies provided," she said, and Camila and Gaby looked at her with anticipation and fear.

"What happened with the guy in the trunk?" Camila probed, scared, as she held Thiago's hand. He squeezed hers reassuringly. Always a supportive gentleman. She's a lucky girl.

"He's in stable condition in the hospital. He took quite a beating, but he's alive. You ladies saved his life. You should be proud of yourselves," Carmen said, and they breathed a sigh of relief.

Gaby played some music. "Now, let's celebrate!" she said. "It's my girl's birthday, not a funeral, thank God!" she added instantly, standing to dance.

They spent the rest of the night dancing. I ordered pizza, and Carmen asked where they'd go next … as if they hadn't been through something disturbing.

Camila and Gaby started naming places they wanted to visit, undeterred by the earlier trauma. Paulo and Thiago were also giving them suggestions.

"The Dominican Republic and Colombia are definitely on the top of the list, but we want to make it special. We were hoping the four of us could go together," Camila said romantically.

"For sure, on the double honeymoon!" Thiago said, kissing her cheek.

"That's a million years from now and may never happen. I say we go after our first semester for spring break!" Gaby suggested. My girl is always a realist and lives in the present moment

Here I thought Carmen would help me reel them in. But instead, she's fanning the fire. I hope the next adventure isn't this exciting, if you know what I mean, although I can't help but feel that someone would've lost his life today if they hadn't been there to witness the incident.

Things work in mysterious ways. They have this incredible gift. Maybe they are meant to use it for good, whatever we perceive this good to be.

There's a saying that not all heroes wear capes. So, perhaps my girls are destined to help people with these gifts.

Even so, I'm selfish. I prefer Camila and Gaby don't help if it requires putting themselves in harm's way or risking exposing themselves.

Sometimes, people need to save themselves by thinking about the consequences of their actions.

When Camila arrived home, her mom was waiting for her with another cake and balloons in the dining room.

"Happy Birthday, my love. You're all grown up, but you will always be my baby. I hope you had a magical day," she said, hugging and kissing Camila.

"Thank you, Mom. I had a great day, more magical than you can imagine," Camila admitted.

Her mother smiled and told her to make a wish. "*Pide un deseo!*"[40] she said, and Camila did. Camila ate her third piece of cake of the day. She certainly has a sweet tooth.

"Happy Birthday, Princess!" her father said, coming into the dining room, picking her up, and twirling her around like a small child.

"Papi!"[41] Camila protested, "I'm *an adult now*," she said, smiling.

---

[40] Make a wish.
[41] Daddy

"Mi reina, tu siempre seras mi niña!"[42] he said, putting her down and handing her an envelope.

"What's this?" she asked, taking it.

"It's a birthday gift. From Mom and me," he said, going over and wrapping his arm around his wife's shoulders.

Camila's parents looked at their little girl with love and pride, who was not so little anymore, as she counted the bills in the envelope.

"Wow!" Camila said, surprised. "That's a lot of money!" She ran over and hugged them. "Thank you. I love you," she said emotionally.

"Well, it's a little something to get your adulthood started. Spend it wisely, *y busca un trabajo!*"[43] Mama Bear said, smiling at her. Camila gave them another hug and ran up to her bedroom.

Gaby, guess what? she thought.

I know you're wondering, but they don't have automatic access to each other's thoughts. They have to grant further permission for this to occur. They can call on each other with their thoughts, but the other person can ignore it, sort of like rejecting a call.

Gaby didn't answer. *I wonder what she's up to*, Camila thought while Gabriela was making out with Paulo in his car. She had left her cell phone in his car, and he went to drop it off.

"Can't you teleport over here or something? What's the point of having that cool superpower if I have to drop the phone off?" he complained when she called his house to tell him.

"Stop being lazy. You're three streets away. Come, and I'll make it worth your while," she teased, and Paulo laughed.

"I'll be right there, ma'am!" he said, ending the call and sprinting away toward the door as Thiago looked on, jumbled.

"I'll be right back," he said to his brother.

"Where are you going?" Thiago asked as he ran off.

"To see Gaby," Paulo shouted on his way out.

"Lucky you!" Thiago shot back sadly.

He wanted Camila to spend the night with him but didn't ask. I always say you will never get what you want if you don't ask for it. You can't expect others to read your thoughts, at least not all the time.

---

[42] My queen, you will always be my little girl.
[43] And get a job.

Thiago was also sad that he didn't get to spend the day with Camila as he wanted. He planned to cook for her and have time for them, and unfortunately, he didn't have an opportunity to give Camila the gift he got her with all the turmoil that transpired.

Gaby was waiting for Paulo outside. Her parents weren't as strict as Camila's, but she knew not to cross the line. So she got in the passenger seat.

"Thank you, handsome," she said, taking the phone and kissing him.

"Why don't you guys spend the night? I think Thiago would like that," he told Gaby.

"Why do you say that?" she asked him curiously. "I mean, I'd love to spend the night!" she said, kissing him again.

"I think Thiago feels bad that you guys went off to Puerto Rico. He had this grand day planned for Camila's birthday," Paulo said, feeling bad for Thiago. However, Paulo hoped he could make Thiago's night, or rather have Camila do it, with Gaby's help.

"He can do it tomorrow or the next day. No big deal. I told her we could go after, but she insisted. It's her birthday, her choice. I had nothing to do with it. I don't want him to think I'm coming between them," Gaby said defensively.

"He knows you were first," Paulo said, laughing. "There is no coming between the two of you, that's for sure," he added. "Just do it for me, please, and for him," he said, winking at her. "I'll make it worth *your* while," he said persuasively.

"Anything for you, baby!" Gaby said, kissing him a third time. "I think Camila wants to talk to me," she said, taking a deep breath.

"Cool, just go to her house, and I'll see you at our place?"

She nodded and gave him one last kiss. "See you later, alligator," she said.

"In a while, crocodile," he responded and backed out of her driveway.

Gaby watched him drive away and hurried up Camila's front steps. Camila's father answered the door.

"Hey, Gaby, what's up?" he asked her.

"Hi, *tío*,"[44] she said, rushing past him. "Spending the night with Camila. I hope you don't mind!" she said, halfway up the stairs.

"Gaby's sleeping over?" his wife asked, coming out of the kitchen.

"Yup!" he said, and they laughed. "I should've gotten those bunk beds a few years ago when you suggested it," he told his wife, following her to the kitchen.

"*Yo te lo dije, y no me hiciste caso!*"[45] she said as he hugged her.

"You in here?" Gaby said, opening the door. Camila was changing into her pj's. "Got something a little sexier?" Gaby asked with a frown, and Camila looked up at her, puzzled.

"What you have in mind?" Camila asked.

"Oh, nothing," she said, sliding her fingers over Camila's vanity and walking back and forth intriguingly.

"What is it?" Camila asked anxiously. "Spill it!" she demanded.

Gaby smiled, showing a mouthful of teeth, and sat on the bed. "Girl, it's still your birthday. Don't you want *one* last gift?" she asked, wiggling her brows up and down. "Let's spend the night with our handsome, hot, and very sexy boyfriends," Gaby suggested, and Camila laughed.

"Girl, you don't have to convince me or be all mysterious about it," Camila said. "You just have to say the word, and I'm out," and they both laughed.

Suddenly, Camila's bedroom door opened. "Good night, girls," Camila's mother said and quickly walked out.

"Good night!" they yelled so she could hear it.

"Let's go to Paulo's room. I want you to surprise Thiago," Gaby said, taking Camila's hand.

"Your wish is my command!" Camila replied, and they were gone. But as I said, you never know a thing for sure until you ask!

Paulo jumped, startled as they appeared. "Man, it's hard to get used to that. You two better be careful you don't give someone a heart attack," he said, his hand over his chest.

Gaby sat on the bed next to him. "Poor baby." Then she kissed him, and Camila hurried out.

---

44 Uncle
45 I told you, and you didn't listen.

Camila tapped softly on Thiago's door and heard him walking to it. He opened it and pulled her in with excitement. "You didn't say you were coming," he said, kissing her.

"I wanted to surprise you!" she smiled.

Don't shake your head. The details don't matter. What's important is that she's there.

"I have something for you," he said, going to his nightstand and taking a small gift box.

His room was very plain. Thiago still had a twin-size bed. His small room was crowded with a TV stand, a computer desk, and one nightstand. Some still half-peeled superhero stickers were on his walls. I guess he and Camila have one more thing in common.

"What is it?" she asked as he handed it to her.

"Open it!" he said, and she did.

"Wow!" she exclaimed, removing a beautiful ruby heart pendant on a gold chain from the tiny box.

Thiago must've spent all his savings on the lovely gift. He was very thoughtful and deeply in love with Camila.

"Thiago, this is beautiful!" she said with teary eyes.

"You have my heart. I just wanted to give you a physical representation so you never forget it," he replied, and she hugged him.

"I love you forever!" she said, and he whispered, "I do too."

Camila and Gaby were in Camila's room early the following morning. They showered and got ready to spend the day with Thiago and Paulo. They were talking excitedly when Camila's mother walked into the room.

"You two are up early," she said as she noticed they were dressed and ready to go.

"Ma, remember we have volunteer work to do," Camila reminded her, and she smiled.

"That's right. I'm proud of you ladies," she said, leaving the room. She doubled back as she saw the necklace around Camila's neck.

"That's lovely. When did you get that?" she asked Camila, pointing at the pendant.

"It was a gift. From my friend Thiago," Camila confessed.

Her mother wore a thoughtful expression. "He has good taste," she said, shutting the door.

"Aw, I feel guilty," Camila said when she was gone.

"Oh, please, let's go," Gaby said.

They left the room, and Gaby gently pushed Camila down the stairs so she would hurry.

They were going to spend the day at an amusement park with the boys. Like I said before, the boys will be going away at the end of summer, and the girls wanted to spend as much time with them as possible.

So one day, they teleported to a different country, and the next, they teleported to the boys, and everyone was happy.

"Good morning!" Camila and Gaby greeted us the next day at my botanica. They were there bright and early.

"Good morning, ladies," Carmen said.

"How did it go yesterday?" I asked.

"We had a lot of fun. Long lines for the rides, but still fun," Gaby said, taking a piece of candy from a bowl by the register and popping it into her mouth. How kids can eat candy at any time of the day is still a mystery to me.

"I found a park near the Colosseum in Rome. It looks like a good place to pop up," Carmen said to Gaby and Camila. "You'll be able to see the Colosseum from there. It's within walking distance," she assured them. Gaby and Camila looked at each other and grinned.

I looked at the three of them, utterly lost. *What the hell?* I thought.

"Sounds good!" they said. "Anything else we should know before we go?" They looked at Carmen, and she shook her head.

When did Carmen become Alfred for the Batgirls? I'd also like to know if she is researching these locations for them. I hope they don't expect me to do that when she leaves.

"Have fun and be careful. If anything happens, don't hesitate to leave. Who cares who sees," I said, still scarred from the last trip. "Walk around holding hands to be safe," I recommended. They laughed, and Carmen did too.

What? I have to make sure they are okay. They seem to attract a lot of trouble. Call me crazy, but I don't care if someone exposes Camila and Gaby at this point. I only wanted them to be safe and return in one piece.

"*Parco Celio!*"[46] the girls said as they waved.

They were thinking about a place in the park with no people. They thought being specific couldn't hurt, and neither did I.

When they arrived, no one was there. Finally, the girls turned and saw the majestic Colosseum. They skipped eagerly in its direction.

The weather in Rome was excellent ... warm, not hot. The sun shone brightly, making it a perfect day to explore.

The park was beautiful, with green grass, tall trees, blazing flowers, and stone benches. They expected something smaller with less vegetation, but this was a pleasant surprise.

They walked around in awe of this ancient city, rich with history. The Colosseum is a marvel. They admired its greatness and the ancient sites around it. They continued and walked for a long time, taking it all in.

Finally, they arrived at Vatican City. "They have a museum!" Camila said gladly.

"Let's go into the church first," Gaby said, and they stood in line at St. Peter's Square. They looked around with amazement. It was a beautiful square framed by a large colonnade extending from the basilica and opening into a large, curved shape surrounding the main square.

Once inside, they admired the art and the architecture. The *Pietà*[47] caught Camila's eye, and she stood before it feeling moved. The sculpture depicted the body of Jesus on the lap of his sorrowful mother, Mary, after the crucifixion. Camila was not a mother, but she couldn't fathom the pain and agony that Mary went through at that moment.

The details of the work of art are incredible. For example, Camila could see the ribs and adnominal muscles on the body of Christ and the folds and creases on Mary's draped clothing.

It truly was astonishing. How the artist could chisel this so magnificently onto a piece of marble was remarkable in her mind.

Tears of gratitude and joy rolled down her face. She felt privileged to be there to admire such an incredible piece of art. *I wish Thiago were here to see this*, she thought. Thiago loved art.

---

46   Heaven Park
47   The Piety, which is a work of Renaissance sculpture by Michelangelo Buonarroti, housed in St. Peter's Basilica, Vatican City.

Gaby stood beside her and held her hand. This gift allows them not just to see the world but also to appreciate it. It is truly a precious gift, and I wish everyone who can travel would do more of it.

It was getting late. The girls had already spent much time admiring the art, but Camila wanted to see the Sistine Chapel, so they made their way there.

Although the exterior architecture was breathtaking, the frescoes that decorated the walls were most impressive, but the ceiling undeniably took the cake.

They were captivated. No photography was allowed, and Gaby was trying to sneak a picture when a security guard called her out for it, so they rushed out of the room.

"Are you trying to get us arrested?" Camila asked her as they hurried away. Gaby just laughed.

As they walked, they noticed two men that looked oddly suspicious. They were carrying an artifact that looked priceless.

One man had an eagle tattoo on his neck. They quickly disappeared into a room that was roped off to the public, but the girls thought nothing of it.

"I'm hungry!" Gaby said.

"There's still so much we haven't seen," Camila whined.

"Girl, this is too much for one day. We can come back whenever we want—ten more times if you want to, but right now, I need food!" Gaby proclaimed, pushing her.

"OK, let's find a bathroom or something. I can't walk anymore," Camila said. So they went into a restroom, held hands, and teleported out. They popped up in an alley near Fiori Square.

They walked for a while and found the statue of Giordano Bruno. Then they asked a passerby to take a photo of them standing beside it. Well, Camila did. She's a bit of a nerd.

Bruno was tried for heresy by the Roman Inquisition and burned to death in 1600 by the church in that very square where his statue now stands.

"You're such a geek!" Gaby told her. "Come on. I'm starving!" she said, pulling Camila away from the statue.

They saw a few restaurants. Finally, they decided on Taba Café and sat outside to enjoy the beautiful cobblestone square with street performers and lovely people. The sun was setting as they looked over the menu.

They ordered a bottle of red wine and everything on the menu. "This is the best food I've ever had. Nothing back home tastes like this. This food is delicious!" Camila raved, savoring everything. "Umm, this is so yummy. I want to try everything they have!" she told Gaby heartily.

Gaby nodded in agreement with her mouth full. A lady leaving the restaurant stopped at their table and told Camila, "I love how you eat. You eat with such passion!"

Camila smiled and replied, "This is the best food I've ever had!" Smiling, the lady walked away.

They also had dessert and eventually finished the bottle of wine. "Today was truly amazing!" Gaby happily exclaimed.

"I could do this the rest of my life!" Camila replied. I guess if we could, we all would.

"Yeah, but if you keep eating like that, you'll need *two* jobs. Thank God we have no other expenses," Gaby said, and they laughed.

"A toast to seeing the world and stuffing our faces," Camila said, and Gaby nodded in agreement.

"There is no way I'm walking to a park or whatever. Let's find an alley and get out of here," Gaby suggested.

"Amen, sister!" Camila seconded, and they walked down an empty street, holding hands. If anyone saw them vanish, they'd think it was a mirage because it was already dark.

That "adulthood" money will go fast if they continue to eat like that.

"We're back!" they said happily, and I was glad to hear the joy in their voices. They seemed relaxed.

"Good. Any incidents?" I asked.

"Nope!" they answered.

"Tell us all about it!" Carmen eagerly encouraged them.

"It was incredible!" Camila said, "but there was so much more I wanted to see and do. A few hours was not enough. So much history and art, it was fascinating," she continued. Gaby shook her head as Camila talked about art and architecture.

"She should get a job at a museum or something," Gaby told me, giggling.

"Oh, and this one," Camila said, pointing at Gaby, "almost got us arrested!" After stating that, she folded her arms.

"When I asked about any 'incidents,' getting arrested would make that list," I say.

"Stop exaggerating!" Gaby told Camila.

"What did she do?" I asked, laughing.

"She was trying to take pictures inside the Sistine Chapel," Camila informed us. Carmen and I laughed, and Gaby joined in.

"I would've done the same thing," Carmen said. "You two can go back whenever you want, but that's a once-in-a-lifetime trip for some," she added.

I hope Camila and Gabriela know exactly how lucky they are.

EPISODE SIX

The media have been covering the greatest heist in modern history all day. It appears Vatican City was the target. The authorities are not disclosing what the perpetrators took during the robbery, but there is no way it could have happened without inside help.

The Corps of Gendarmerie is investigating in partnership with local law enforcement and Interpol. They are asking anyone with information to come forward.

"The girls were there yesterday. Do you think they saw something?" Carmen asked me, and I looked at her with dread crawling up my spine.

"I hope not!" I said, texting Camila to see if she's seen any of this on her phone.

They were conducting a serious investigation, asking anyone who was there and could have seen something to come forward.

Unfortunately, this robbery at the Vatican spelled terrible news for the girls since they were there the day it happened.

What if they were on close caption TV and were found and questioned regarding the robbery? I knew that an incident-free trip was too good to be true.

"They will probably scrutinize all video footage of that place from the last twenty-four hours and want to interview everyone there!" I told Carmen, visibly agitated.

"So what? They were only visiting," she said.

I don't think she comprehended the severity of the girls' situation if they get interviewed about being present on the day of the heist.

First, you cannot just waltz into the Vatican and steal from the Catholic Church. They will leave no stone unturned to find out who did this.

"They will find the culprits. I only hope my girls don't get caught in the crosshairs," I said, and Carmen just shook her head.

"How could this possibly affect them?" she asked.

"Carmen, they have no travel records. So, how do we explain them being there in the first place? Camila and Gaby will be deemed a threat to National Security, not just here but internationally," I replied, terrified.

Carmen shook her head again. She didn't think what I said was of any concern.

"Can you imagine if governments knew that people were capable of teleporting? Then naturally, they would try to use them as weapons by any means necessary," I said.

"I don't think it will be a big deal. How can those girls be a threat to anyone?" she asked me, not in the least worried. I swear, if she had a kid, it would be a clone of Gabriela.

"We know that, but no one should have those abilities. The people in power will say they can go into 'classified places,' and you already know how *that* goes," I stated.

"Let's not count our chicks before they hatch. The girls would've told us if they had witnessed something, and we would've alerted someone," she assured me. I nodded, trying to keep calm.

"Besides, no travel records mean no way of identifying who they are!" she offered comfortingly.

I wanted to believe she was right. Then Camila texted me back. We are on our way.

They had gone to the beach by Rye Playland. They need to go to a country with beautiful beaches. It is beyond me that they can go in the cold water on our shores.

The doorbell rang, and I already knew it was them.

"What's all this about the greatest heist in history at the Vatican?" Camila asked me, still at the door.

"How about you get in here, and we can quietly talk about it?" I said, pointing at a customer with my head. They act like what they do is normal and no big deal.

Hispanics not only point with our fingers, but we also suggest with our mouths and heads. In fact, any suitable body part will do. I've used my foot to point something out. Anyway, let's carry on.

They filed in, and I told them to go upstairs. "Carmen, can you please see if they need something? I'll be closing soon," I said, and she nodded. So the four followed Carmen to the house.

When I finished with the customer, I closed up. I smelled cigar smoke and saw Lazaro had come out for air.

"*Ahora es que la cosa se pone buena!*"[48] he said with a smirk, walking past me.

I stared as he walked away but didn't say anything.

"Going out. Don't wait up, sis," he informed me and left.

I stood there for a while, unsure if he meant it in a good or bad way. I could always ask, but I'd rather not. I'm not ready to consult with him on this matter yet.

When I got upstairs, the television was on. The newscasters continued their coverage of the heist on all the major channels, and Camila and Gaby kept exchanging nervous looks.

"OK, I'll address the elephant in the room. Did you guys steal something from the Vatican?" I asked bluntly.

Camila and Gabriela looked at me, horrified. "How could you suggest something like that?" they replied, affronted.

"Yes or no, ladies?" I asked again. They shook their heads and sucked their teeth.

"Idelfonsa," Camila started, "how could you think something like that? Sure, I can see why you would feel Gaby could commit a crime, but she would never, and neither would I!" Camila concluded indignantly.

I wanted to believe she was telling the truth, but when we care about people, we tend to see the best in them and think of them as incapable of certain things. However, I've learned through the years that we never truly ever know a person, so I wanted to be sure because that would be a disappointment equivalent to heartbreak.

"All right, I just wanted to be sure to know how to proceed," I said, sitting.

"What, you a lawyer now?" Gaby asked.

"Why? You guilty?" I asked in return. She didn't respond.

---

[48] Now is when things start getting good.

We continued to watch the news. Mainstream media have few updates, and the reports are vague. An unknown person or persons removed a priceless object. The authorities were uncertain if it was an inside job, and the case was still under investigation.

"What do you think it was?" Thiago asked no one in particular.

"Probably something they stole, to begin with!" Carmen said crudely. "The church possesses a treasure trove in possessions, most of which was ill-gotten," she added bitterly.

It doesn't matter now. Two wrongs won't make it right, and I doubt whoever took whatever it was planned to return it to its rightful owner. It's all about making a profit in the end.

"Well, we did see two odd-acting characters carrying some partially covered artifact that looked made of gold. The object was rectangularly shaped, but I couldn't identify it from where we stood," Camila said nonchalantly.

"Are you *kidding* me!?" I said, upset, and they all turned to look at me. "You didn't think that was worth mentioning when the news broke?" I asked, livid.

"For all we know, it could've been two employees moving an item. Of course, if you're going to steal something, you should go for the exit. But instead, they went into a roped-off room inaccessible to the public," Gaby added defensively.

Unreal! So they *did* see something after all. Now, what should we do? I mean, do we call the tip line? If so, what do we say?

This incident was too much. I knew leaving the States was a terrible idea from the beginning. But if they're on video near the suspects, it's only a matter of time before this catches up with the Teleporting Teletubbies.

They witnessed the theft of what I believe to be the Ark of the Covenant and didn't tell anyone.

"So, should we call the hotline?" Camila asked, now with some concern.

"I don't know, Einstein. What do you think?" I asked sarcastically. She rolled her eyes. I felt like slapping her over the head like she was my kid.

"Wait a minute. Didn't you say they don't have travel records? So, what are they going to say?" Carmen asked. *Now*, she wants to act like a real adult.

"We could do an anonymous tip, like in Puerto Rico," Gaby chimed in.

"I don't know, baby. The Vatican robbery is next-level grand theft. I don't think an 'anonymous tip' will fly," Paulo tells her as he puts his arm around her waist.

Silence filled the air for a while as we watched the same report repeatedly on every channel.

"I have an idea!" Thiago said as if he had just discovered a new element for the periodic table.

"Is that so?" I asked skeptically. I'm running out of faith that they'll have any good ideas.

"Why don't you call and say you two are psychic and you had a vision of the incident, and give them a description of what you saw!" he stated animatedly.

Like I said, nothing to see here. All out of ideas.

"I don't know. But of course, that would put the girls on the radar," Carmen said restlessly.

"The CIA and other agencies liked to consult psychics back in the day. Have you ever heard of Project Stargate?" Thiago asked. None of us had any idea what he meant.

"I think it's a great idea!" Carmen said again, not helping the situation.

"Let's try it. We can say we astral project too, and that's why it seems like we were there," Gaby added.

They are just full of ideas today, aren't they? And none of them are any good.

"Don't volunteer any astral 'whatever' ideas if they don't ask you. I think you need to go home and sleep on it. If you decide to go ahead with this, make sure you have your story straight. We're not in Kansas anymore, Dorothy," I told them, and everyone laughed.

I wasn't trying to be funny, but it seems I'm hilarious.

"Whatever," I said as I noticed no one attempting to leave.

"Get out of here, all of you. I know you'll be back at the crack of dawn," I said wearily, waving my hands. This ordeal had been exhausting. I needed to sleep it off, and so did they.

"*Ay, comai,*[49] don't kick them out like that," Carmen said compassionately.

"You want to go with them?" I asked, and she laughed. I know she secretly loves this nonsense.

"You heard the woman. Get out of here!" Carmen declared, trying to help me.

"Fine, but we'll be back real early. Shit, we might teleport at the crack of dawn!" Gaby reported, and we laughed but knew she was not lying.

"Honey, you're going home. I need my bed to myself. You kick in your sleep," Camila told her as we headed downstairs.

"Please sleep in late. Enjoy your vacation," I pleaded as I opened the door to let the kids out.

"You can sleep with me," Paulo told Gaby.

"Don't tease me with a good time!" she replied, and they giggled as they got into the car.

I hope they sleep in and consider cautiously what they plan to do about what they witnessed.

"You two think you will get into trouble if you come forward with what you saw?" Paulo asked on their way to drop off the girls.

"I don't think so," Gaby responded. "It's not like we stole anything," she added, leaning on Paulo's shoulder.

Camila looked back at them, seeing Gaby so relaxed that she refrained from adding what she was thinking.

"Tell your mom you're staying at Idely's because you have to do something early and stay at my place," Thiago begged Camila.

"Yes!" Gaby jumped in her seat and shook Camila's shoulders.

Camila didn't answer right away. Instead, she was in deep thought about the heist.

Why is it that something happens every time we go somewhere? she wondered. Camila felt strongly they were supposed to call this in and that the purpose of their gift was to help.

"Sure," she said, dialing her mother to inform her that she would

---

[49] Oh, girlfriend

not be spending the night at home, and Gaby followed suit while Thiago happily drove to his house.

Camila rested her head on Thiago's chest, listening to his heart beating softly and deep breathing while sound asleep. *Hey, Gaby, you there?* she thought, and Gaby responded immediately.

Yeah, what's up? Camila heard in her head.

I can't sleep! she confessed.

Me neither, Gaby admitted.

I think we need to call the tip line and inform them what we saw at the Vatican, Camila stated.

I knew that you wanted to do that, and I agree. I support whatever you want to do. We did nothing wrong; we'll be all right, Gaby responded, and Camila felt her yawn.

OK, go to sleep. We'll figure this out tomorrow, Camila told her.

Camila and Gaby fell asleep, and I prayed through the night. I have a bad feeling about this and hope it doesn't expose them to anything harmful.

The next day, the girls were at the botanica extra early.

"We've decided what to do," Camila started. "We'll call in an anonymous tip and see what happens," she finished, now somewhat unsure.

"Good," I stated. "I just hope they'll take the tip and not want to talk to you ladies any further," I said, still convinced this was a bad idea.

I know they think they have a handle on this, but the truth is, there is no telling what will happen once they open Pandora's box.

Camila called the tip line and informed the person on the other end that two suspicious males were carrying a concealed object, one with a tattoo on his neck, and that they had entered a restricted room.

When asked to leave a number in case someone had further questions, Camila declined.

"You know they know exactly where you placed this call from. If anyone has more questions, they *will* find you," I informed them.

"I did my part," Camila replied. "Whatever happens beyond that is out of my control," she added.

"Where to today?" Gaby asked, and we all looked at her.

"Why don't you ladies sit this one out!" Carmen stated, and I looked at her, surprised.

"Maybe actually give us a hand or do something locally," she added.

That's real mature of her, I thought.

"I don't see what the big deal is. No point sitting around stressing about something we have no control over," Gaby said, disgruntled.

"I agree. Since it's our mission to help, we might need to go somewhere else," Camila added with conviction.

"Mission?" I asked.

What in the world is she talking about with this mission nonsense? But before I could ask for clarification, she gave me a mouthful.

"I feel we have been blessed with our gifts so that we can go to different places and uncover something. We are supposed to help by bringing these things to light!" Camila stated with conviction.

"Okay, Mother Teresa, you want costumes too?" I asked sarcastically. "Now, you're talking crazy," I countered.

If she thinks this is some "mission" for divine intervention, they will *always* run into trouble. That's just how the mind and world work.

"She's right, Idely. We have been allowed to have these abilities, and I don't think we are supposed to sit around scared," Gaby interjected, and I shook my head.

"I think they're both right," Carmen added her two cents, holding my shoulder.

"I know you're worried and scared, but if the girls aren't supposed to be doing this, they wouldn't be able to," Carmen agreed.

Perhaps they're all right, but I can't help but feel that they may run into danger or get caught up in some freaky experiment.

"OK, but I feel they should lie low for a few days. Let's see if the authorities catch these guys," I said to Carmen.

The girls walked to the back and sat on chairs where the saint statues were while Carmen and I continued to talk.

"Hey, Teleporting Teletubbies!" I yelled to them. "How about you lie low for a few days and then carry on with business as usual? Let's see if the tip pans out," I suggested.

"OK," they replied. "Got anything to eat?" Camila asked.

"I have bread. Make a sandwich or something. There is also left-over arroz congri[50] from last night, but it's too early for that," I told her.

"Oh yes! I'll fry some eggs with the rice. It's the perfect breakfast," Camila said hungrily, running upstairs.

"I'm not eating that. I'll make an egg sandwich!" Gaby said, following Camila.

Camila will eat anything at any time of the day.

Soon, the botanica phone rang. Carmen answered.

"Hello, yes, someone called with a tip a little while ago on the Vatican heist tip line, and I'd like to ask a few more questions," a pleasant lady informed Carmen.

"Um, well, this is a business. I didn't call. The owner didn't either, but perhaps one of the customers did. I'll ask around and have them call you back if I can locate them," she replied hesitantly.

I knew that if they had more questions, they would locate the caller or the point of origin for the call. So I'll wait for the girls to eat and come down again before breaking the news.

The girls returned a little while later. "You ladies find your way around the kitchen?" I asked.

"Yup, we stuffed our faces. This one ate all the rice with *two* fried eggs," Gaby said, pointing at Camila, and we laughed.

"Don't judge me!" Camila pretended to pout, smiling.

"No judgment here!" Carmen said to her, and I immediately killed the vibe.

"Someone called back from the 'tip line.' They have a few more questions for the caller," I informed the girls, and Camila and Gabriela's eyes widened.

"I'm not calling back. I said it was anonymous, and there is nothing more I can add. We left soon after seeing the two creeps hiding away in the Vatican dungeons," Camila stated.

What happened to all that "conviction about their mission"? I see that cookie crumble quickly.

"Screw them. Let's go somewhere fun!" Gaby added.

---

[50] Cuban black beans and rice cooked together.

As I said, it's only a matter of time before this catches up. I hope the girls know what they are doing. It's all fun and games—until someone goes to prison or a lab.

"Let's go to South Beach!" Gaby suggested. Camila grabbed her hand. They smiled and were gone.

"I don't know, Idelfonsa. Do you think those people will just let it go, or should we expect another call?" Carmen asked, biting her nails.

"I know they will continue to call until they speak to the caller. It's only a matter of time," I said, looking at her, and she squeezed my hand.

Crowds of people filled the beach, and it was hot. The girls realized they had no bathing suits and looked for a shop to buy some.

They were sweating from only walking around, and the humidity wasn't helping. Nevertheless, it smelled delightful, the restaurants were open, and people ate outside, laughing, and drinking.

When people are on vacation, they forget their troubles and are more present and less anxious.

My girls were no different. They found a shop, purchased bathing suits, and changed. Then they hurried back to the beach. The sun was burning bright as they lay on the beach towels they had just bought to sunbathe.

I heard the bell and turned to see a tall, muscular man with ivory skin, strawberry-blond hair, and green eyes, followed by a statuesque woman with copper skin, round amber eyes, and long brown hair, both in suits. They look very professional … and slightly intimidating.

"What can I do for you?" I asked with a knot in the pit of my stomach.

They proceeded to show some credentials. "We are with the FBI, following up a call from this establishment regarding the heist at the Vatican in Rome," the woman stated.

"Someone called, and we told them that it was a customer, that if we could locate them, we would inform them and call back," Carmen said unpleasantly.

"You didn't have to make the trip all this way just for that," I said, looking from one to the other inquisitively.

"This is a top priority, and we wanted to follow up in person," the male said, looking around.

"I guess anonymous tips aren't allowed," Carmen said with an attitude.

"So, you *do* know the caller?" the woman asked, taking an interest in Carmen.

"Well, if you don't know who called, they didn't say. So, it's pretty obvious!" Carmen snapped back cynically.

"Do you mind if we look around?" the gentleman asked, walking toward the register.

"Not at all. Be my guest," I said, seeing it wasn't a request.

"Is this the phone they made the call from?" he asked, pointing at the cordless phone by the register.

"Yes," I replied, and he looked up at the ceiling.

"No cameras?" he asked, now looking at me.

"Not in here," I said shortly.

"You should get some," the woman added, looking at the books on the shelves.

"I don't think anyone wants to deal with the spirit realm if they come in to cause trouble!" I said threateningly. They didn't answer and continued to look around.

"Since you don't know who made the call, we'll have the phone dusted for prints," the woman stated, standing by the phone. "It's close to the register. I can't believe you wouldn't see someone use it," she added before I could answer.

"Do what you have to do," I replied.

Now that's not what I wanted to tell the little … well … her, but sometimes, what we say can cause more problems than we need.

The phone rang, and I hurried to answer it. "Botanica San Lazaro," I said with a smile.

It was a customer asking if we did tarot readings. I gave her an appointment to come in and speak with my brother Lazaro, then hung up.

"Will this fingerprint business take long? I have a business to run, and I don't want to give my customers the wrong impression," I said coldly.

The man took out a business card and handed it to me.

"We'll call back tomorrow before we return. We hope you can reach out to any customers you think might have placed the call and inform them that we need to speak," he said, heading for the door, and the woman followed.

EPISODE SEVEN

Carmen and I exchanged looks. "I'll text Camila. They need to get back and sort this out. These people are serious, and I don't want any problems," I said, sending Camila a text to return immediately.

"What's the emergency?" Gaby asked as soon as they returned. "I was soaking in some vitamin D!" she exclaimed with frustration.

They looked ridiculous standing there in matching neon-green bikinis, given the severity of the situation.

"Oh, I'm sorry, Your Highness. I didn't mean to disturb your relaxation time in the sun, but two FBI agents were here looking for the tip caller!" I yelled.

"Are you *serious*?" Camila asked, shocked.

"Like a freaking heart attack!" I replied, throwing my hands up in the air.

"I knew they would continue to probe. This is a serious matter, but the Teleporting Teletubbies want to soak up some sun—as if they needed it!" I announced, now placing my hands over my hips.

"Why are you refereeing to us like we're not here?" Gaby asked.

"Because you two don't listen!" I barked back at her.

I'm nervous and agitated. I want this mess to go away. I don't understand how everyone can be so damn calm.

"Why don't we all calm down? Then I'll call the number on the agent's card and take it from there," Camila announced coolly.

Oh, look at that. Camila will call the FBI, and all this will go away! I forgot to mention that they're also delusional.

"What are you going to tell them?" Carmen asked.

"The truth!" Camila said plainly.

I slapped my palm on my face. Camila and Gaby heeded no warnings. They think they know everything and clearly, don't watch movies.

"Not the *whole* truth," Camila added, seeing my reaction. "I'll say we were there and quickly left to get something to eat. I can provide the restaurant information, and my debit card records can corroborate my story," she explained to us like everything was that simple.

"What if they ask when you arrived in Rome or what hotel you were staying in?" Carmen asked Camila, distressed, and I'm eager to hear what she says since she believes she has this figured out.

"Why would they ask that?" Gaby asked. "They want to know what we saw; we'll tell them *only* that. They don't need to know anything else. We are not suspects," she concluded.

"All right, Johnnie Cochran, since y'all have this all figured out, go call those folks because I don't want to see them in my shop again," I said, frustrated.

Calmly, Camila took the card and walked upstairs. "Hello, my name is Camila De Los Santos. I called in a tip, and now I'm told federal agents have further questions," she informed the person on the other end.

"Yes, this is Agent Smith. I want to schedule a meeting in person. Can you come in tomorrow, say nine a.m.?" he inquired.

"Yes, I can," she told him calmly.

"Great, do you have a pen? I'll give you the address," he said.

Camila returned, and Carmen, Gaby, and I looked at her with anticipation.

"So?" Gaby asked as we stared at her.

"So, tomorrow morning, I have to go in person to answer some questions," she replied, relaxed.

"You mean *we* have to go," Gaby exclaimed.

"I was hoping to go alone and keep you out of it. No need to complicate things," Camila said, playing with her hair, and I wonder if she's on something because she is *waaay* too calm.

"No, I'm coming with you. What if we need to get out of there in a hurry?" Gaby asked.

I quickly added, shaking my head, "I *know* you're *not* going to teleport inside a federal building!"

"We are going to do *whatever* we need to do!" Gaby informed me, and I just looked at her without replying.

I'm at a loss for words at this point. They will walk in as witnesses and teleport as fugitives.

"Fine, Gaby, you can come too, but we are not teleporting in there," Camila said with a little more urgency.

Thiago and Paulo arrived, so now it's a party. "What's up, beautiful ladies? What's with the beachwear?" a smiling Paulo asked Gaby.

"You look sexy, baby, but why so serious?" Thiago asked Camila, sensing the mood.

"Oh, nothing much. Your beach bum ladies got called back from soaking up some sun because they happen to be on the FBI's radar," I said with sarcasm and annoyance.

"What?" Thiago asked morosely.

"How?" Paulo asked, opening a bag of chips he had when he walked in. Ironically, it was popcorn, appropriate because this was starting to feel like a movie.

"How?" I asked rhetorically. "Clearly, calling in a tip is how!" I told him, irritated.

I had a bad feeling from the start, and frankly, I'm not sure calling in this tip was such a good idea in the first place.

"Why don't we all go out to eat? Then Idelfonsa can have a beer or two. She seems a little uptight!" Paulo suggested, and everyone laughed.

I chuckled because this kid was something else. Like his girl, he takes nothing seriously, and if *they're* not worried, why should *I* be?

"Listen, if this is my lady and her best friend's last night of freedom, we might as well have a good time," Paulo continued jokingly.

"I hear that, and sleepover at our place!" Thiago offered, winking at Camila.

"Sounds like a great idea!" Gaby responded willingly. I forgot what it was like to live with reckless abandon.

The girls went upstairs to change while the rest of us speculated about their meeting with the FBI tomorrow.

We all went to a hibachi restaurant, where Carmen and I ordered a few cocktails, and we all had endless laughs. Paulo kept teasing that his future baby mama was going off to prison, and Gaby warned him that someone could turn her out in there.

The food was delicious. Since we were a large party, we had a table to ourselves, and thank God for that. Camila was oddly quiet, and Thiago held her hand most of the time. They ordered different dishes and fed each other what they had.

I assumed her being relaxed and calm was a front, but being around Thiago gave her a sense of comfort and safety. I feel she often acts tough for Gaby's sake. It's nice to see that she has someone to lean on and feels protected and safe when she's with him.

The other two clowns have no care in the world. Not even the threat of prison can damper their mood. The four of them are a perfect balance.

Thiago dropped Carmen and me off at my place. "Good luck tomorrow, ladies," Carmen said, getting out of the car.

"Yeah, and don't say more than you need to," I said, following Carmen.

"We won't, I promise!" Gaby assured me.

"Thanks for all your support. We'll clean up this mess," Camila promised, and I nodded. Carmen and I watched until their car disappeared on the horizon.

"You know I've been looking for a helping hand. Why don't you stay with me? The house is big enough, I know you hate the winters here, but you can always go back to Puerto Rico when it's cold," I told Carmen as we walked inside.

"You want a helping hand, huh?" she asked, laughing, "It takes a village to raise kids!" she added as we climbed the stairs, and I chuckled because she was right.

Camila's mother had loosened her grip. She no longer gives Camila a hard time spending the night out. She knows Camila is a responsible girl and feels her parenting job is complete.

What do you think they're going to want to know? Gaby asked Camila in her head as she elbowed a sleeping Paulo for snoring.

Paulo's room was identical to his brother's, although they preferred different colors. And he had posters of bikini-clad models instead of superhero stickers on the wall.

I have no idea. I suppose the FBI wants better descriptions and possibly knows if we heard any part of their conversations. I've been going over it in my head the whole day, Camila admitted, running her fingers through Thiago's curly hair.

Thiago turned and kissed her. *Good night!* she thought, shutting Gaby out of her mind.

"You were quiet all night. You worried about tomorrow's meeting?" Thiago asked Camila as he wrapped her in his arms.

"Yes, of course. But let's watch a movie and hope for the best," Camila said, searching for a movie on the streaming app.

She'd already spent the day worried about this, and now she just wanted to relax.

I spent the night making an offering to my Orisha and wanting to consult with Lazaro. Still, Camila and Gabriela had already expressed that they believed they were the master of their fate and captains of their souls, and nothing or no one could dictate their future.

They were curious about my spiritual practices, and as I told them a bit of it, they said they admired my commitment, but something like that was not for them. I respect that they are out to carve their own paths, not settling for anything already there.

"We can look to the past for courage. Our ancestors endured a lot, yet they persevered, and so can we," Camila said to me once.

"We can harness their strength and wield it as a shield, but what we should never do, under any circumstance, is stay in the past," she said during one of our many conversations about spirituality and our ancestors.

Camila has strong beliefs about her place in the world, and Gaby shares those ideals.

"We cannot continue to victimize ourselves or pity each other. We are powerful, we are free, and our focus should be to build on the foundation laid down for us by our ancestors, and not just survive, but thrive," Camila told me, wondering why I still carried on with the family business.

"Do you do this because you want to or feel you must? Are you afraid the spirits will punish you if you walk away? And if so, are you free?" Gaby asked me once.

Tough questions, but the truth is that I love my faith, and doing what I do is a delight. However, I understand their need for freedom and the ability to choose for themselves everything in life.

We inherit every aspect of the things we experience, from the food we eat, the music we listen to, the religion we practice, our political inclinations, and our biases and prejudices, and we never question them. So, I'm glad the girls are willing to come up with their own conclusions.

"We are here in the 'new world'; our task is to create something new from the old bricks. It doesn't matter what this 'new' looks like, as long as we can make it our own, so long as we can redefine ourselves and lose the internal identity struggle," Camila said during a conversation with Gaby and me.

"Those of us who are descendants of enslaved people, indigenous peoples, and other marginalized groups are often not enough African, indigenous, and certainly not European. We don't have to prove anything to anyone or need to seek acceptance or validation. Instead, we need to love and accept ourselves," Gaby said emotionally.

"Yes, and go forth and forge a new path. We are all intricately connected on various levels, and regardless of how much we enjoy pointing out our differences, the truth is, we are all human," Camila responded lovingly.

"Forget what people think, and fuck what anyone says. We need to know where we came from, but only *we* can decide where *we* want to go," Gaby added, and we all laughed.

I was worried sick, but I believed my girls would get through tomorrow unscathed. They are witty, intelligent, and with good heads on their shoulders. They had this … I hoped and prayed.

The following day, Gaby and Camila were up early. They wore black slacks. Camila had on a beige shirt, and Gaby wore a white blouse.

They were too edgy to eat. "I want to teleport there," Gaby whined.

"No!" Camila scolded.

"It's cool," Thiago said to Gaby. "I'll take you, ladies." Paulo was still sleeping.

"I'll stay home and have breakfast ready when you get back," Paulo told Thiago on the ride home the night before when he suggested taking the girls in the morning.

Paulo didn't want to get up early. But I hope he has food ready when they return, or there will be hell to pay.

"Thanks for the ride, babe," Camila told Thiago with a kiss when they arrived at their destination. They struggled with the city traffic but made it right on time.

"Call me when you finish so I can come to pick you up," he said out the window.

"Nah, we'll find our way home," a winking Gaby informed him.

Thiago looked at Camila for confirmation. "It's OK. We'll be fine. See you later, my love," Camila said, blowing Thiago a kiss, and he drove off with a salute.

"You ready?" Camila asked Gaby, who nodded. The girls made their way into the building, full of nerves.

The yellow brick road ended, and they were about to meet the Great Oz.

They were greeted and escorted to an interview room, like the interrogation ones you see on TV. But what the hell do I know? So, let's see what happens.

Why does it feel like we're about to be interrogated? Gaby thought, and Camila shrugged.

"Hello, I'm Agent Smith, and this is my partner, Agent Jackson." The same two agents that had been in my shop introduced themselves.

"We were only expecting one person …" Agent Jackson said, and Gabriela immediately replied rather rudely.

"I'm Gabriela Hernandez. I was there with Camila and felt I should also be here." At least she kept it professional and didn't swear.

"Well then, I'm glad you could join us!" Smith said as he and Jackson took seats at the table across from the girls. It was a sterile-looking room. The large table with a glass wall was very plain.

"Let's see," he said, sifting through papers in a file.

"You can start by asking those extra questions you had," Gaby said rudely.

"Ah, yes, I just wanted to read through your initial statement," Agent Smith stated, looking up at them.

"It wasn't that long of a statement!" Gaby pointed out, maintaining eye contact.

I thought she would let Camila do the talking, or at least tone it down a little, but no, she will play hardball like she has a law degree.

Calm down! Camila thought, and Gaby smirked.

"We saw two men carrying a concealed object. One had a tattoo of what appeared to be an eagle on his neck," Camila disclosed before he could answer.

"And they went into a restricted area. What else did you want to ask?" Gaby added. The agents looked at each other quickly, and then Agent Jackson took over.

"Is there anything else you remember? Did you hear them say anything?" she asked them.

"No," Camila answered.

"We were hungry and on our way out to grab something to eat," Gaby added.

"Did you see anything outside that seemed out of the ordinary, like a vehicle or something unusual?" Jackson asked them.

"It's St. Peters Square! It was crowded, and we were in a hurry," Gaby told her, flustered.

"Where did you go eat?" Agent Smith asked.

"How is that relevant to the heist?" Gaby snapped.

Are you fucking kidding me! Camila thought, and Gaby told her to let her handle it.

"You two OK?" Jackson asked, giving them a weird look.

"We didn't have breakfast, and we get cranky when we're hungry," Camila quickly said before Gaby could unload further insolence.

She wasn't lying. Those two are like toddlers. When they don't eat, they throw tantrums. I only hope Gaby doesn't overdo it.

"Is there anything else? We have somewhere to be," Camila asked politely.

"Who else did you travel with?" Agent Jackson asked.

Now, we are entering dangerous territory.

"It was just us," Gaby said coldly and got up from her seat. Camila followed her lead.

"I hope you catch whoever did this," Camila said, standing.

"Wait, I just have a few more questions," Smith stated, pointing at their seats.

"Are they related to the two people we just described because that's all we have! Anything else is irrelevant, and if you want to ask personal questions, we'd like an attorney present since now it feels like an interrogation and not a good faith questioning!" Gaby stated, and Smith looked over at Jackson.

I don't know what she made up, but my girl is quick on her feet. Hopefully, that brings whatever this is to an end because things can only get hairy from there.

"If you don't remember anything else, that will be all. You've already signed in, and we have your information. If there is anything else, we'll be in touch," Agent Jackson said, standing and extending her hand.

The girls shook her hand and quickly headed for the door.

"Those two are strange and hiding something," Jackson told Smith once they were out of earshot. The agents followed them out to the hallway.

"Do you think it has anything to do with the heist?" Smith asked her.

"I don't know. It could be something trivial, but something is up with these two," she said as they watched them walk unusually fast toward the elevators.

"It could be nerves," Smith responded as they observed them enter an elevator.

"Nope, there is something more to it. I can feel it!" Jackson said, convinced that they were hiding something from them.

That was close! Camila thought, afraid to speak aloud.

I had it! Gaby thought, and Camila gave her a death stare.

No, psycho! You almost blew it! Camila thought, still looking at her.

"Whatever!" Gaby spoke aloud now. "Let's get out of here." So they walked a few blocks, saw a train station, and made their way down the stairs.

"This is too crowded," Camila said, looking at everyone. The girls didn't visit the city often and were unfamiliar with public transportation.

They walked upstairs and down a few more streets. Finally, they saw a construction site, sneaked behind some Porta-potties, held hands, and disappeared.

I heard something upstairs and then footsteps coming down the stairs. I told them they couldn't just pop up in the botanica like that. What if I had customers?

"How did it go?" Carmen asked immediately.

"It could've gone better, but Gaby will be her charming self anywhere," Camila replied, rolling her eyes, and Gaby shrugged her shoulders.

"Let me guess. The politeness just oozed out of her with ease," I said sarcastically, and they laughed.

"So disrespectful!" Camila stated, still laughing.

"Oh, please! I got us out of that mess. They were about to start asking questions we could not answer, and when I mentioned a lawyer—problem solved. Thank you very much!" Gaby said proudly.

"That's smart!" Carmen praised her, impressed.

"I don't care how you two did it. I wanted you to get out of that without attracting any attention to your ability and return safely," I said, thankfully.

"Never! I had the whole thing under control. I saw right through them. Good thing I went. Mother Teresa here would probably still be babbling or telling them how we teleported there," Gaby remarked, poking Camila in the ribs.

"Shut up. I just have a different approach, but I'm *not* an idiot!" Camila told her, insulted by the assumption.

"Right! Anyway, I'm starving. We are so used to coming back here that we forgot the boyfriends are making us breakfast," Gaby reminded Camila.

"That's right!" Camila exclaimed, taking her hand. "We'll be back later!" they said and were gone. I hope that's the last we hear from Agents Jackson and Smith, but I can't help but feel uneasy.

The girls were back in Thiago's room. Seeing he wasn't there, they ran downstairs to the kitchen. "We're back!" they sang together.

The boys were busy in the kitchen, and the girls joined them, sitting on the stools by the kitchen counter. Then, finally, Thiago and Paulo came over and kissed them.

"How did it go?" Thiago asked.

"Easy peasy—thanks to me!" Gaby said triumphantly, and Camila rolled her eyes but was too hungry to argue.

She let Gaby have her five minutes of glory as she told the boys about the meeting with the FBI agents.

"That's my girl!" Paulo said pompously and gave Gaby another kiss. Thiago and Camila laughed.

"You'll tell me the *real* story later, right?" Thiago asked Camila in a whisper.

"Yes!" she said, kissing his cheek.

They had breakfast and spent the rest of the day at a nearby park. I hope they catch the culprits soon, and this whole heist incident is behind us. That was a close call.

Agent Jackson placed Camila and Gabriel's names into a law enforcement database on a hunch. After that, she will receive an alert if the girls are involved with law enforcement ever again.

EPISODE EIGHT

A few weeks passed, and the media announced the capture of two suspects they were looking for but gave no further information. They thanked the public for helping with the capture but said nothing else.

"Good!" I told Carmen, and she nodded in agreement. "I hope we don't have to hear anything else about this case," I said as I handed her a cup of coffee. I made toast for us to enjoy with it.

Like me, Carmen doesn't like to eat heavily in the morning. Instead, we want to have a big lunch. We had quite the appetite when we were girls, just as Camila and Gaby do today, but we need to watch what we eat these days.

"I don't know. This whole thing seems shady. It's like they don't tell the whole story. Everything is a big mystery," Carmen stated, taking a sip from the mug the girls brought her from Rome. They got one for me too. That was one trip they didn't return from in a hurry.

"The only reason they let this out to the public was that they needed help catching the perpetrators. If not, we would've never known. The church has always been secretive and shady. And if you ask me, that was an inside job!" I asserted as I took a bite from my toast.

"Yeah, they probably stole from themselves to make an insurance claim. God only knows how much the 'allegedly stolen' object is worth. But they have so many lawsuits that they probably want to make up for it some—"

"Good morning," the girls announced as they arrived. They startled Carmen midsentence, and she spilled coffee down her shirt.

"*Me cago en ná.*[51] I still can't get used to that," Carmen said, wiping her shirt with a napkin.

"*Coño.*[52] I'm sorry. Take it off. I'll wash it in the sink," Camila said, guilt-ridden.

"No, honey. It's OK. You'd think I'd be used to the two of you popping in unannounced, but it's freaky every time," Carmen said, going to change.

"Maybe if they didn't show up at the crack of dawn while we're still half-asleep, we'd be better prepared," I yelled after her as if the girls were not standing before me.

"Good morning to you too!" Gaby said, taking the other half of my toast off my plate.

"How did I get stuck with you?" I asked, and she kissed my forehead as she sat across me.

It was just Lazaro, my parents, and I growing up, and this kitchen felt huge. These days, it feels like it's too small.

I have a six-seat dining set. Good thing I never downsized after my parents passed away because now I'm considering purchasing one with eight chairs. "Oh, you love us," Gaby smirked with a mouth full.

"What else you got?" Camila said, opening the refrigerator.

"What do you want?" I asked, getting up, and Camila closed the fridge door to sit next to Gaby at the table.

The girls think they live here, but the truth is I don't mind. I like having them around. They're like family.

"Surprise me!" Camila said with a big, innocent smile.

"Pancakes, eggs, and bacon are what I'll make. That's it!" I said as I sprang into action like an unpaid butler.

"Yummy!" they happily exclaimed, and Carmen joined us, wearing a clean lavender shirt.

"Give me a hand, sunshine. The kids we never wanted are hungry!" I said, and the girls laughed.

Carmen quickly joined me without complaint. She liked the girls, and I don't blame her. What's there not to like? They're amazing.

"The boys are at campus today. It's an open house for first-year

---

[51] Holy shit!
[52] Damn!

students. They will show them around before they move in. We're thinking of surprising them there," Gaby said as Carmen and I prepared breakfast.

"No, *you're* thinking about it. We should give Thiago and Paulo some space and go somewhere else exciting!" Camila said, playing some game on her cell phone and not looking up. Gaby gave her the side eye.

"I think Camila's right," Carmen said. "Give them space and go to Paris!"

I elbowed Carmen.

"I say you go to that campus and mark your territory, ladies," I insisted, hoping staying local would keep them out of trouble.

"You just don't want us going on international teleports!" Camila told me. That girl knows me too well.

"You're right. Give those boys space and go check out your own university," I admitted as I poured pancake mix into a frying pan. The bacon was sizzling away in another pan, and the smell was making me hungry.

"That could be fun. We can spend the day in the Big City!" Gaby said enthusiastically.

"Fine!" Camila said, defeated, not wanting to argue about it because Gaby can be annoyingly persuasive.

She didn't want to go to MIT because, as the summer ended, she was more determined to break up with Thiago.

Please don't ask. We will get to that later. There are a few weeks of summer left, and that's not important right now; back to the matter at hand.

"Will you be going there like regular folk, or are you—" before I could finish, they answered the question in unison.

"We're teleporting!" they said, and we laughed. But, of course, they are. Why wouldn't they?

One can only hope they learned a lesson from the Vatican incident, but wouldn't you travel anywhere that way if you could teleport? I know I would. I'm just being overly protective at this point.

We enjoyed breakfast, and I made some peppermint tea, and once done, they were off.

"Stay out of trouble!" I yelled as they waved goodbye.

For the love of God, please stay out of trouble, I thought. If they get into anything else, I will sage their asses.

"*Ay Dios!*[53] I don't know how much more my heart can take," Carmen said with a hand across her chest as we watched them vanish. I understood what she meant because I felt the same.

"*Estamos muy viejas para esto!*[54] I said teasing, and Carmen shoved me.

"Speak for yourself. I'm still a spring chicken," Carmen retorted, and I burst out laughing. "Age ain't nothing but a number and a state of mind," she told me.

After a huge breakfast, we will have to start jogging because we are no spring chickens. We're grown hens! I thought, feeling satisfied.

"*Sí, cómo no!*[55] I replied, and we made our way down to the shop.

Lazaro had already opened and was waiting for us to come down, smoking a cigar, and drinking black coffee.

Camila and Gabriela agreed they would teleport to an empty women's bathroom at NYU. The precision with this is essential. They certainly can't afford to attract any more attention to themselves.

My biggest fear with their gift is them popping up and someone seeing them. Could you imagine? I know I don't want to. It would be nice if invisibility came with it.

Hopefully, there is more to come. Maybe this ability is some mutation, and more powers will emerge over time. Although, as Carmen says, I don't know if my heart can handle any more excitement.

They arrived in an empty bathroom, as desired. Gaby opened the door and poked out her head, noticing an empty hallway.

"Come on," she said, pulling Camila out of the bathroom. "Let's walk around!"

When I said they should go check out the campus, I didn't mean it literally. I was hoping Camila and Gaby would go into the city and check out the neighborhood and see the local shops and places to eat, but they went to see a college building. Not fun, in my opinion, but whatever ... back to it.

---

[53]   Oh God!
[54]   We are too old for this.
[55]   Yes, of course.

Just as they exited the bathroom, they heard someone screaming, "No, bro, please, don't kill me!" It was a young man pleading for his life.

Unfortunately, the hallway was dark, and they saw no one they could alert for help.

Camila instinctively grabbed Gaby's arm and crept toward the voices. *We should be getting the hell out of here!* Gaby thought in protest, but Camila shook her head.

The air smelled like rubbing alcohol, and the building was warm. Maybe building maintenance was conserving energy and keeping the air-conditioning running low.

Gaby, let's go. We are here because we are supposed to help, Camila thought, walking faster.

Now, you already know what I'm feeling, right? I mean, come on! Get the hell out of there already! I don't usually agree with Gaby, but she's the one with some sense in this situation.

"Where's my fucking money?" they heard the man demand.

There was a painful whine, and a man replied, "I'm going to get it. I just need more time!" He was crying now.

Camila and Gaby crept closer to their room. The door was ajar, and the room had poor lighting.

"Your time is up, bitch!"

At that point, the girls could see into the room.

The assailant raised his knife, and Camila screamed, "Stop!" But the act was already in motion, and unfortunately, the homicidal maniac stabbed the poor boy's hand he had raised to protect his face.

The attacker ran out of the room, and the girls bolted back to the bathroom. They shut the door and held hands.

By the time the attacker reached the bathroom, they were gone. He stood in the hallway scratching his head but was distracted by the young man he had stabbed who was running away.

He followed him but still thinking about the girls. Maybe they had gone into a different room, but that was unimportant now. He had to catch his prey. He would find those girls later and make them pay for their intervention.

"Oh my God, oh my God," the girls said as they arrived in my living room, hearts racing and mouths dry.

They were petrified and sat on my sofa, still holding hands. I heard murmuring upstairs, followed by the screaming of my name.

"Idelfonsa!"

Carmen looked at me, scared. I motioned for her to go upstairs while I rushed to lock the door. I swear these girls are going to put me out of business. Carmen ran into the kitchen to grab a water pitcher and some glasses.

"What happened now?" I asked as I saw them pale-faced on the couch.

They stared at me, blinking rapidly, still in shock. I sat beside Camila and Gaby, and Carmen placed the glasses on the coffee table in front of the sofa and filled them up.

"Drink!" she told them, and they each took a glass of water and gulped it down like they had just returned from the Sahara.

Now, I'm convinced that no matter where they go, they will always run into something because they go looking for trouble.

"We need to call the police," Camila said, still breathing heavily.

Clumsily, she reached into her pockets, looking for her cell phone, but couldn't find it. "Shit, where's my phone!" she yelled, frustrated.

"Take mine," Gaby said, handing her cell phone to Camila.

Shaken, Camila took it and made the call. She reported a stabbing inside an NYU building but wasn't sure of the exact address. Finally, she described the attacker and ended the call.

Then she handed Gaby her cell phone. "I'll call your cell to see if it's somewhere in here," Gaby said, hoping they'd find it.

Fortunately, the victim got away, but the assailant returned to the scene to search for the girls. However, there was no trace of them. He was beginning to question if he had even seen them or if the cocktail of drugs he was on was causing him to hallucinate.

While rushing out of the building, he found Camila's cell phone on the hallway floor near the bathroom. The phone was locked, but her screen saver was a picture of her and Gaby.

"Gotcha!" he said, putting the phone in his pocket, glad this verified what he saw.

Camila's phone vibrated in the perpetrator's pocket. He took it out and saw a picture of Gabriela.

"Hello, sunshine!" he said, and a stunned Gaby did not answer. She could only breathe heavily.

"Why don't you tell me where you and your friend are hiding, so I can return her phone," he said sweetly.

Gaby ended the call with no reply. She was as white as a ghost as she slowly turned to look at Camila.

"He has your phone," she said softly, sinking into the sofa and covering her face with her palms.

"Who does?" Camila asked, peeling Gaby's hands off her face, desperately hoping it was not who she was thinking.

"The dude with the knife," Gaby said, confirming Camila's suspicion, and Camila looked at her with dread.

Camila held the stare but didn't verbalize what she felt, and I wondered if they were telepathically communicating or simply talking with their eyes.

No one said anything for a long time. "Okay, let's think. Why don't we do that 'find my phone' thing, and get a location to inform the police where this son of a bitch is!" I suggested.

"I'll get my laptop," Carmen said, sprinting to the bedroom.

Camila and Gaby remained silent. I texted Thiago and told him what had happened. I instructed him not to call or text Camila's phone.

I hope Mama Bear doesn't call her. That would make things worse.

Thiago was frantic since he was out of state, but I assured him that Camila was well and that we had already alerted the police, but he demanded to speak to Camila.

That boy is intense. He's crazy about his girl. I don't know how that breakup will sit with him, but that's for another time.

"I think he'll dump the phone," Gaby whispered after a while, and we looked at her expecting her to go on.

"He's a criminal. He knows the police will track him with it," she said in a normal voice, and we all nodded.

It made sense, but now he knows who they are. So, he'll surely come after them if he's not apprehended.

Camila kicked off her sneakers. She was sweating, and I immediately got up to turn on the air conditioner.

The pink tank top she wore stuck to her skin, and she held her curly hair up in a ponytail.

Remember when Camila said helping was their mission? Well, I wonder how she likes them apples now? So, who's going to help save these heroes?

Agent Jackson received an alert from the law enforcement database. Camila De Los Santos placed a call from Gabriela Hernandez's phone about a stabbing in an NYU building in Manhattan.

She noticed a follow-up call stating that the perpetrator had taken Camila De Los Santos's cell phone.

"Listen to this. Our wonder buddies, the ones with the confirmed heist tip from the Vatican, just popped up on my radar again!" Jackson zealously informed Smith.

"What do you mean 'popped up on your radar'?" Smith asked her, muddled.

"I put their names in the law enforcement database and got a hit. I told you something is unusual about those two," she said, searching for the incident on her computer.

"Local PD found traces of blood at one of the campuses, but no victim," Jackson said, rubbing her chin.

"No victim, no crime!" Smith stated, looking over his case files.

He had no interest in the girls. To him, they were just two snotty teenage girls who happened to be at the right place at the wrong time.

On the other hand, Jackson was a bloodhound, and she was tracking the girls' scent. So I only hope she can let it go and stop monitoring them like they're some common criminals because when you go looking ... you're likely to find something.

"Don't you find it strange that they witnessed yet another crime?" Jackson asked Smith.

"I could care less about those two. That Vatican case was not our jurisdiction, and I'm glad it's over," he said, uninterested.

"Well, I don't believe in coincidences. There is something here, and I'm going to figure it out!" she said determinedly.

"Knock yourself out, but we have plenty of work to do, so I suggest you grab a file and get started," Smith said, laughing, and she rolled her eyes.

Thiago called Gaby's phone a third time to speak with Camila. "Everything's all right!" she assured him, suggesting he return to what he was doing and stop worrying. "I love you too!" she told him sincerely before ending the call.

She felt a pang of guilt considering breaking up with Thiago. She truly loved him, and he was terrific, but the distance wasn't something she could deal with, and she wanted him to feel free and enjoy his college years as a single man. So she refuses to be apart from him, worried he's hooking up with other girls.

"Let's go get you a new cell phone. You still have plenty of 'adulthood' money left," Gaby told Camila, and Camila nodded in agreement.

"Yeah, it's going to have to be at least three models old if we want to keep eating!" Camila said as she put on her sneakers.

"Don't worry, sugar mama. I have some savings left," Gaby reminded her.

They headed down the stairs, and I told them to stay out of trouble and hurry back. I didn't want them roaming around with a maniac on the loose. All their shenanigans were going to give me an ulcer.

They found the local branch of Camila's service provider and bought the least expensive phone. But first, Camila told the clerk she needed a new sim card because someone had stolen her old phone.

Technically, that's not true. The girls went minding their business, and Camila lost her phone in that process, but that's a side point. Let's continue.

The young man assisting her informed her the sim in her old phone will be deactivated, and the person in possession of it won't have access to her information.

"Too late!" Gaby said aloud, but he only looked over at her and continued, not understanding her reference.

"Whatever," Camila said mostly to herself as she waited for the polite clerk to finish.

When the transaction was completed, he handed Camila her new and ready-for-use phone and a business card. On the back, he wrote his name and number.

"Call me if you need anything," he said to her with a warm smile.

"Thanks, Andres," she said, returning the smile.

She and Gaby left, hurrying back to my shop, looking over their shoulders as they walked, making sure no one was following them.

"You think he can figure out where we live with just our photo?" Gaby nervously asked Camila.

"I doubt it," Camila replied, hoping it would keep Gaby calm, but the truth is, she felt with the internet that anything was possible.

When they arrived, I relaxed. But my nerves had my stomach in knots knowing there was a homicidal psychopath who wanted to harm them.

"Call your mother," I told Camila, hoping her mom hadn't already called her phone, and in that instant, I had a frighting thought.

"*Santa Barbara Bendita!*"[56] I shrieked. "What if that motherfucker spoke to your mom, and she gave him your address to return the phone, not knowing what's going on?" I said, and everyone immediately panicked.

Carmen started to pray a Hail Mary in Spanish, Camila and Gaby uttered many swear words, and they disappeared before I could reel them in.

Now I know why they advised against yelling "fire" in crowded places. Had this been the case, the frightened mob would've trampled me.

I paced back and forth between aisles, from the cash register to the door, making promises to my Orisha. Carmen was on her knees, praying the Lord's Prayer. I could not make this shit up if I tried. Sometimes, reality is stranger than fiction.

"*Ay, comai!*" Carmen said, standing and holding my hand. "Should we call the police?" she asked me, antsy.

---

[56] Blessed Saint Barbara!

I went over to the counter and texted Gabriela. "Is everything all right over there?"

"Let me see what she said. Then if she doesn't reply within the next five minutes, we'll go over and call the police," I said calmly.

"The girls should tell their parents about their ability; they can't continue to keep it from them. It could be dangerous," Carmen said, afraid.

"We've discussed it briefly, and they feel the parents shouldn't know. I'll revisit that conversation with them, but for now, let's hope everyone is OK," I said, impatiently awaiting a reply.

EPISODE NINE

Camila and Gabriela were in Camila's room. They stood quietly for a while, trying to decipher what they heard.

"*Luna, tú qué lo ves …*"[57] They heard a song by Ana Gabriel playing faintly.

"I think it's coming from the kitchen," Gaby whispered, and Camila nodded in agreement.

They held hands and softly walked to the door. Opening it, they peeked out into the hallway. The coast was clear, so they headed out.

Camila thought they should sneak out the front door, then come back in, pretending to have just arrived. Explaining to her mother how they got in there would be challenging and made her doubtful because she's not easily fooled.

Okay! Gaby thought, following Camila's lead.

"*Luna y dile que vuelva porque ya es mucho …*"[58] They heard Camila's mother singing as they made it down the stairs.

The girls walked as fast as they could toward the door when they heard Camila's mother.

"Camila?" Mrs. De Los Santos asked, bewildered. The girls turned around to see a puzzled Mama Bear.

"When did you get home? I didn't hear you," she asked Camila suspiciously.

"We, um, we—" The doorbell rang, and Camila ran to get it, with Gaby close behind.

Of course, Mama Bear followed. She didn't understand what was happening but was determined to find out.

---

[57]   Moon, you who see him.
[58]   Moon and tell him to come back because it's too much.

"Why do you look so pale?" I asked Camila when she answered the door.

"What the hell is going on?" Mama Bear yelled from behind Camila, her hands firmly planted on her hips and brows raised.

"Camila invited us over for dinner!" Carmen blurted out spontaneously.

I smiled, grateful for the save but restless at the same time. This evening will prove to be interesting. What conversations will we have? We're all already on edge from the incident at NYU.

"I forgot to call you earlier and came in ahead to see if you were cooking enough," Camila lied.

"There is always enough. Your grandma taught me to cook as if always expecting guests," she said, motioning us to enter.

In Hispanic culture, we often cook twice the amount needed for the head count in the household, just in case we have neighbors, friends, or relatives drop by. Therefore, there are always leftovers, and they taste better too.

"I'm making locrio de gallina con tostones, y ensalada de aguacate,"[59] Mama Bear said as we followed her into the home.

She accommodated us at the exquisite mahogany dining table and offered us something to drink.

"I'll take rum and Coke!" I said with a little too much excitement.

A strong Dominican rum will help me get through this. Carmen took a beer, and Camila and Gaby joined us at the table.

"Make yourselves at home. I'm glad you're here. I don't get to see Camila much these days!" Mrs. De Los Santos said and then excused herself to finish up in the kitchen.

"Everything OK?" I asked as soon as I was sure Mama Bear couldn't hear us.

"Apparently," Camila said, shrugging her shoulders.

"What do you mean?" I asked, unsettled.

"Well, we got caught and were saved by the bell!" Gaby chimed in, sticking up for her girl as usual.

"Caught?" Carmen asked, lost, but before either of the girls could answer, Mama Bear returned.

---

[59] Rice and chicken cooked together, twice-fried plantains, and avocado salad.

"Here you are," she interrupted, bringing the drinks.

"Thank you!" Carmen and I said, sounding like the girls.

El que anda con cojos al año cojea![60] I thought and smiled. Mama Bear smiled in return, and I took a gulp from my glass.

She left again, and I asked for clarification. "We were sneaking down the stairs, and she caught us red-handed right before you rang the bell, but I think that sorted itself out," Camila explained.

"Did you ask her if anyone has called about your phone?" I inquired, still concerned about the lunatic after them.

"No, lady, as I said, we got here not long before you did and were trying to sneak out when you arrived," Camila replied.

Great, so basically, we are sitting ducks at this point.

"You need to tell her about the teleporting. Things are getting crazy now," Carmen said warily.

"No!" Camila objected. "That's off the table. She'll lose her mind, think I've been doing it all along, start bothering me, and possibly want me to see a doctor …" she trailed off, shaking her head.

"That's not a good idea. Mama Bear tends to overact," Gaby added.

"At least tell her you misplaced your phone and ask her if anyone has reached out to return it," I insisted.

"Okay," Camila replied, seemingly ruffled. I shouldn't be scared if she's not afraid for her life.

"Camila!" her mother yelled, and Camila rushed to the kitchen.

"Yes?" Camila asked her once there.

"Help me set the table."

"Oh, by the way, I lost my phone today. Did anyone call or come by to return it?" Camila asked her mother calmly.

"How did you lose your phone? And why would anyone return it?" her mother inquired.

"I must've dropped it, and you never know. There could still be good people out there," Camila said, glad her mother hadn't spoken to Michael Myers, the infamous slasher.

"No, honey, I'm sorry, but no one has called or stopped by the house with it. I'm afraid whoever found it must've kept it, and let me

---

[60] The one that walks with the lame in a year limps.

be the one to tell you that, sadly, there is no good left in this world!" she added gloomily.

Camila assisted her mother in setting the table and bringing out the food. Everything smelled good and looked delicious. I couldn't wait to dig in. All this adrenaline rush made me hungry.

We ate, and I complimented Mrs. De Los Santos on her cooking. Then Mama Bear asked what the girls were doing for me, and I said it was primarily inventory and digitizing how the business operates.

"They came up with the idea for a website," I lied after my second drink. Boy, that rum is strong!

"That's great. The girls are brilliant. I'm glad they're doing something productive this summer instead of wasting time on the internet. It's good that they are helping you incorporate it into your business. It has helped us greatly with ours. Caby Movers is doing amazing," Mrs. De Los Santos told us enthusiastically, and I felt remorseful that we were lying to her.

That would be a good idea, though. I do need to get with the times at the botanica.

We spent more time chatting with Camila's mother. Again, I complimented her on her taste in décor, and she eagerly inquired if I wanted to see around the place. I happily obliged.

Finally, Carmen and I excused ourselves for the evening and thanked them for a delicious meal and a lovely time. I was glad that Carmen came up with that idea. It was nice getting to know Camila's mother.

"See you ladies tomorrow," I said as they waved from the door with a bright smile.

"Crisis adverted, my friend—for now," I told Carmen as we got into the car.

She insisted on driving, and I didn't argue. I was fine, but she only had half the beer, and it's important not to drink and drive.

"I'm glad you came up with an idea so quickly. You saved the day, and I feel that now that Camila's mother has got to know us better, she'll feel more comfortable with Camila spending time at the botanica. I think people fear what they don't understand," I said.

"Yes, I got the same vibe. Camila's mom seemed more relaxed. Now, let's see what new adventure tomorrow brings!" Carmen stated with nervous laughter.

"I hope they fly up to the moon and chill there a while," I joked.

"For what? So they can discover the alien base there, and then NASA comes after them?" Carmen expressed a little too severe for my taste, and I cracked up.

"Please, stay, my friend. I have truly missed you!" I told her genuinely.

"Seriously, but do you think it's possible?" Carmen asked me gravely.

"If what's possible?" I questioned.

"That they can go to the moon? They haven't thought of going there—" I cut off Carmen.

"Nena," I said to her. It's the pet name I called her when we were girls. "Please don't *ever* mention that to them—like *ever*!" I cautioned. Could you imagine? Yeah—no!

It is plausible that they can very well go to the moon with their ability, but that probably wouldn't be safe, so I wouldn't even mention it.

Gaby would probably convince Camila, and they're lost in space the next thing you know.

"Gaby is spending the night," Camila said to her mother.

Am I? Gaby thought.

"Okay!" Mama Bear yelled from the kitchen.

"Come on!" Camila said, rushing up the stairs, practically dragging Gabriela.

"What's the urgency?" Gaby asked as soon as they were in Camila's room.

"I need to go see Thiago now!" Camila declared.

Huele a peligro![61] But let's see what this is about, shall we?

Gaby looked at her skeptically. "That seems impulsive," she said carefully, sensing Camila was on edge.

"What happened to waiting for your mom's good night?" Gaby added, stalling.

---

[61] It smells like danger.

They just had a pleasant evening, and Gaby didn't want to mess it up because of Camila's current unhinged behavior over God knows what.

"I want to speak to him, and I fear it can't wait. Screw my mom!" Camila stated.

"This seems vital since you're willing to risk a blowout with your mother. What is it that you urgently want to discuss with him?" Gaby asked, hoping she would tell her now rather than later.

Gaby knows Camila and feels this is something she should probably discuss before making a rash decision. Camila was very controlled and rational, but she occasionally acted impulsively.

"He's over there, all concerned about me here, not properly focused or engaged with what he should be preoccupied with, and I don't think it's fair. I need to set him free!" Camila said, her voice shaking.

"Oh, wow, you want to go through with that?" Gaby said, sitting on the bed.

"Why wouldn't I? I mean what I say!" Camila responded bitterly, standing by the bed and looking at the wall.

"Because you love him," Gaby added.

"Yes, I do, and that's exactly why I want to do this," Camila admitted, restless.

Gaby felt there was a whole lot more bothering Camila. Maybe she's having post-traumatic stress from what happened at NYU and didn't know how to express it adequately.

"Cami, that makes no sense to me. I think you're just afraid of what you feel, and you'd rather break up with him to protect yourself from getting hurt eventually," Gaby informed her, taking her hand and pulling Camila down onto the bed beside her.

I'm impressed with Gaby. Those are my sentiments exactly. Love can be challenging to navigate when you're young, and it can be terrifying to feel so deeply about another person.

"I'm so tired of feeling like I have to do things following a certain script!" Camila yelled out.

"What is it you're so frustrated about?" Gaby asked, unsure why she was so upset.

"Everything!" Camila exclaimed intensely, and Gaby just stared at her, prepared to listen.

"Like really, fuck the patriarchy in the sense that women have had to fit into a mold for far too long. Every aspect of our being is always under harsh scrutiny," Camila barked, crossing her legs in the lotus position. Gaby looked on so that she could get whatever was bothering her off her chest.

"Take, for example, my decision to end my relationship with Thiago. He's excellent. I love him more than our limited language can express, and I know I'll always love him, but I want him to be free. I don't want to be apart worrying about what he's doing and vice versa. If we are each other's destiny, we will find our way back to each other, and if that makes me a bitch, then I accept it, but I will not be sorry. And I most certainly won't explain myself to anyone," Camila snarled.

"I don't think you owe anyone an explanation. I simply want you to think this through so that you don't regret it later," Gaby said softly.

"Idelfonsa told me something similar. Hold on to it if you have something good, but I'm tired of constantly being told what to do," Camila said to her.

Before I go on, I'll give full disclosure. I'm old school, but I'm not for this alleged "patriarchy" they like to blame on us. Camila should know that. I never married or had children as society dictated. If that's not an act of rebellion, I don't know what is!

I just see real, true love in Camila and Thiago, and the truth is, the first love is the real deal. After that, the others come along to help us forget, and the goal then is to find a friend we are attracted to so they can accompany us through life.

I only want her to understand what she has, to see its greatness, and hold it with both hands because life might just come along and pry it out of her grasp.

I can't live for her, though. No one can. So she's going to have to figure this out on her own.

"Is there something else bothering you?" Gaby asked, squeezing Camila's hand for encouragement.

Camila had bottled up many emotions, and the day's events triggered her.

They did go through something pretty traumatic. I feel they don't correctly process these incidents emotionally. So instead, they bottle up things, pretending everything is fine.

We all do that, but we need to learn to manage our emotions healthily, or else they'll creep out of us in ugly and destructive ways.

"A lot is. It's probably that time of the month or the near-death experience, but I'm just annoyed. Another thing, my mom keeps asking when I'm going to get my hair done as if it's not acceptable when it's curly," Camila said scornfully

"You know how your mother is. She thinks it looks better when you straighten it, that's all. So I wouldn't even sweat it. It's a cultural thing for her," Gaby reminded her.

"I'm afraid I have to disagree with it. That standard of beauty is incredibly narrow and part of a patriarchal system that has survived and thrived this long due to the number of women in its corner allied to it. It's astounding," she replied to Gaby forcefully.

"If you deviate from the script, you're attacked by women! Men won't openly do it; it is the women. Men simply ignore it and go for their preferences. We are our worst enemy, and we are ruthless. It's exhausting!" Camila argued, and Gaby agreed.

"Women do too much for beauty and acceptance—hair down to our toes, everything has to be 'perfect.' Even the aspect of our genitalia has to follow a script. We cannot look different or operate outside the prescribed model," Camila continued, and Gaby nodded in agreement.

"I say let women do whatever the fuck we want. Let's not condemn other women if that girl doesn't want to shave any part of her body; cool. Suppose that the other girl wants to shave her head. Great! If anatomically she is different, celebrate it! Enough with one size fits all already. The rainbow has many colors, so you can admire your favorite instead of saying how much you hate red," Gaby added.

"Exactly! This system bleeds into our perception of self and how we behave and manage our relationships. As women, we must walk on eggshells, not too loud, unable to freely express ourselves for fear we might get categorized as angry, bitchy, difficult, or whatever else outspoken women get condemned of," Camila continued to rant.

"Yeah, remember that time last year when Tanisha was telling us about her relationship with Marcus, and she confessed she had never had an orgasm but always pretended to so as not to hurt his feelings? Can you imagine the number of dissatisfied women out there because they're afraid to tell a man how to do it?" Gaby recalled.

"Tanisha is doing him a disservice. It's all new to them, and instead of helping him be better, she sits there and lies because women have had no voice for far too long. So I refuse to comply!" Camila said proudly.

"I've been listening to you, and believe me, I'm in your corner, but the truth is, Thiago is not the 'patriarchy,' and he is wonderful, and most importantly, he loves you! So, if you want to go ahead and break up with him, fine, but wait for them to come back, please," Gaby pleaded.

"And by the way, wear your hair however you want. Don't let that bring you down. Your mama doesn't know any better. That's what her mother told her, and she thinks that's what she's supposed to tell you. So you break that cultural curse by not conforming, and if you ever have a daughter, you make sure to never, ever bring that up," Gaby added.

Lately, I've agreed more and more with Gabriela. She is right. I believe what is happening with Camila is due to the intensity of her feelings for Thiago. She's afraid. Afraid of heartbreak, she's bracing herself by trying to get ahead of it, and I don't blame her. It hurts and hurts bad, but that's life, and all of it is worth living and experiencing. It's better to have loved and suffer heartbreak than never to share what she has with Thiago.

This little trip to MIT most likely brought the whole thing front and center, and she's probably already aching with longing. He hasn't even been gone that long. Imagine when it's for extended periods. It'll be agonizing.

Pain should not discourage us from living. On the contrary, it should fuel the flames for life, for it is fleeting, and if we can truly understand that, we will have a different perspective. Then things would lose importance, and we would take more risks.

"Today was stressful. I'll get some sleep and see how I feel tomorrow," Camila said, crawling to her pillow and under the blanket.

Gaby patted Camila's feet as she watched her assume a fetal position and hug her pillow.

"You want to be alone?" Gaby asked Camila.

"No, it's OK. You can stay," she replied.

Gaby changed into her pj's before getting into bed. "It's OK to miss him, you know. You don't have to fight it. Feel what you—"

Camila interrupted Gaby before she could continue.

"You can stay, but only if you shut up!" Camila mumbled into her pillow, and Gaby threw the shirt she'd just taken off at her head.

"So rude!" Gaby said as she got into bed beside her. Camila must be in her feelings because she's never rude.

"Can I say one more thing?" Gaby asked Camila.

"No!" Camila groaned.

"I'll say it anyway. You were fearless today. I admire you very much because I wanted to get the hell out of there, but you did what's right and saved that kid's life," Gaby told her emotionally.

I think they're both brave. Camila and Gaby bring out the best in each other. We need to surround ourselves with people who make us better and those we admire and want to grow with us, never people who drain us and make us feel bad about ourselves.

"You're brave to sunshine because you're always there with me. Thank you for always having my back. I wouldn't be brave unless I knew you were there with me. I'm brave because of you. I love you," Camila told her, a single tear rolling down her cheek.

There it is. Excuse me while I blow my nose. All we need to do is talk it out and love it out. It is essential for mental health to say what we think and, most importantly, express how we feel to those around us. The girls make me proud.

"Good night!" Camila whispered.

Good night, Gaby thought, leaving Camila to her thoughts.

Those internal struggles are often excruciating. Our mind tells us to do one thing, and our heart screams for something else. So, here's a word of advice: always follow your heart.

No matter what Camila decides, we will support her. It's her journey; only she knows what's best for her. Camila knows what to do in her soul, and whatever that is, it will be for her highest good.

None of us can know what she needs. We can try to advise her, but this is her life to figure out. All we can do is love and support her.

EPISODE TEN

armen and I finished our coffee and went down to the botanica. We had just opened and were dusting, getting ready to
receive customers. Then suddenly, I heard the bell jingle, and
the door opened.

"Good morning," I heard and turned around to see Agent Jackson
strolling in like she was strutting down a runway. She was alone. I guess
her partner didn't want any part of this.

"Crime never sleeps, I take it," I said as she reached me by the
register and removed her flashy sunglasses. She was wearing jeans, a
floral shirt, and sandals. It must be her day off.

"It's a friendly visit. I was just in the neighborhood," Jackson said,
leaning on the counter with a devious grin on her face.

I look at her nervously. I'm sure she wasn't just "in the neighborhood," but she smiled, I assume to make me feel comfortable.

"Are the best friends forever around?" she asked, glancing around
discreetly.

She's so predictable. She dresses down and struts in, pretending to
have been in the neighborhood, but instead, she's here stalking Camila
and Gabriela.

"No, why? What's up?" I asked, uncomfortable.

The Vatican heist is old news. I can't understand why she's here and
what she wants with the girls. This woman is obsessed.

"I heard about an assault they witnessed at an NYU building.
Just wanted to make sure they're OK," she mentioned casually, and I
immediately didn't like where this was going.

How did she know the girls witnessed it?

"Really? I didn't know that the FBI got involved in petty crimes,"

Carmen said, rolling her eyes and snapping her neck.

If Carmen keeps that up, she'll have a stiff neck. She certainly doesn't hide her disdain for Agent Jackson at all. She might as well tell her she's not welcome here while wearing an "I hate Agent Jackson" T-shirt.

"Well, from what they described, it spells attempted murder to me and far from petty," Jackson replied snarkily.

However, I agreed with Carmen and would like to know when the FBI follows up on petty city crimes.

Finally, and most importantly, why does she know specifically that the girls witnessed it? Something isn't adding up with this surprise "friendly" visit.

"It's disconcerting that they witnessed another crime within weeks from the last, don't you think?" Jackson asked us cynically and stared at us obnoxiously.

"I think it's more disturbing that you have come here to harass two young girls for no reason," I countered bitterly.

She knew this wasn't about her concern for their well-being but her need to be correct.

"I'm just concerned for their safety. If Ms. De Los Santos and Ms. Hernandez keep this up, it will only be a matter of time before one or both of them get hurt," she continued, striking a chord.

"Listen, lady, I think you should mind your own business. Go do some *real* work!" Carmen told her angrily and stomped to the rear to dust the statues, ranting in Spanish as she went.

Then we heard footsteps rushing down the stairs. "Good morning!" Camila and Gaby sang in unison.

Great! Now, these two show up while their law enforcement stalker is still here.

"What's *she* doing here?" a defiant Gaby asked, seeing Agent Jackson standing by the cash register.

"Minding her business!" Carmen yelled from the back, rattled and rolling her eyes.

My mother used to say if you roll your eyes too much, you will end up crossed-eyed, and I smiled as I noticed Carmen get more agitated now that Camila and Gaby had arrived.

"I was just curious about the incident at NYU," Jackson admitted getting straight to the point and walking around the counter to better look at Camila and Gabriela.

It seemed like she was sniffing for blood. This woman is relentless. Aren't there any from the most wanted list she could be working on instead of being in my shop investigating innocent teenagers?

"What does that have to do with the FBI?" Camila asked, calmly sitting on a stool in front of the counter, legs crossed and arms folded as her orange star-studded summer dress draped to the ground.

"Nothing. I only care about your well-being. But if you keep running into trouble, it's only a matter of time before one of you gets hurt," Jackson warned her.

Midnight, my black cat, jumped on the counter and hissed at Jackson, who immediately moved away from the counter.

"Thanks for your concern, but we can take care of ourselves," Gaby replied, standing beside Camila, showing a united front.

"Do you ladies live here?" Jackson continued to encroach. I told her the girls weren't here in the botanica. I never said they weren't upstairs at my residence.

"Agent Jackson, thank you for your concern, but we can take care of ourselves, as Gabriela already stated. If there is nothing else you need, and since you're not on official business, I will have to ask you to leave. We have work to do," Camila told her politely.

That's my girl! Sometimes, I don't think she has it in her, but she does. Although I'll admit, it's all about tact. You can send a person straight to hell, and they won't object if you do it with diplomacy.

"Okay, I'll go, but I want you to know that I know something is going on with the two of you. I came as a friend. I hope you know you can trust me. I'll be watching either way," Jackson warned them and left.

"Whatever!" Gaby stated after she exited.

"I know, right? That woman has some nerve. She's probably illegally spying on you ladies. You should report her," Carmen suggested walking back to the front counter.

"That's a good idea, Carmen. Jackson is not supposed to be keeping tabs on us like *we're* criminals," Gaby said ardently.

"Let it go. We don't need any more problems. Jackson can watch us all she wants. We're not doing anything wrong," Camila counseled Carmen and Gaby.

"I agree. Stay out of trouble, and you'll be off her radar," I said. Yet, I'm starting to believe that trouble finds *them*.

"Reporting crime is not an offense." Gaby protested, aggravated.

"Neither is teleporting, but we keep it from her and make her suspicious," Camila added.

I hope this girl isn't suggesting we tell the "good" agent about teleporting. But if she is, Camila has utterly lost her mind.

"Are you implying we tell her about it?" I asked, concerned.

"No, not exactly. I can understand where the agent is coming from, that's all. She's in law enforcement. She's supposed to be mistrusting, and we are lying, so we shouldn't be too hard on her," Camila said sympathetically.

My girl is wise. She always tries to walk a mile in the other person's shoes. We can learn a thing or two from her. Being kind is about trying to understand the other person's perspective. She is correct. We have not been forthcoming with Agent Jackson, so naturally, she doesn't trust us.

They spent the rest of the day at the botanica. Carmen and I didn't ask if they had plans to go anywhere for fear that they do and that something terrible would happen. But on the other hand, I think Agent Jackson's visit might have shaken them up because they stayed put.

Gaby pulled me to the side to tell me about Camila's meltdown the night before. "She's under a lot of stress," I told her.

I still don't completely understand her obstinance with this breakup. "If it ain't broke, don't fix it!"

"The two of you have been dealing with a lot, coupled with all the changes that are coming with the new school and the boys going away," I said, placing my hand on Gaby's shoulder, and she nodded in agreement.

"I can't imagine any of this being easy, but I'm proud of you, Gaby. Everything you said to her is what I would've said. You're becoming an exceptional young woman," I told her, beaming with pride.

Carmen went up to the house to prepare dinner. I turned the sign on the door to *closed*, and the girls and I went upstairs to help her.

"I'm making trifongo con chicharron!"[62] Carmen exclaimed with excitement.

"Yes!" the girls shouted as they sat at the dining table with cups of limeade.

Thiago and Paulo will be returning this evening, and I sensed that Camila was tense in anticipation. Gaby, on the other hand, was giddy with excitement. I wonder why?

"Oh my God, this is delicious," Camila said as she dug in.

"Yeah, I prefer trifongo to mofongo," Gaby added with a full mouth, and we all laughed.

"I'm glad you ladies like it. Food always makes you feel better, especially when you make it with love," Carmen told them.

"Thank you, Carmen. We love you too," the girls exclaimed as they continued to enjoy their meal.

Carmen was right. Enjoying a delicious meal with people we care about brings a troubled mind comfort. I know firsthand the girls have a lot on their plate and are under a lot of stress.

After dinner, Camila and Gaby decided to walk home. It was a beautiful summer night, and they wanted to enjoy the last days of summer.

"Go straight home; no funny business," I warned them as I opened the door to let them out.

"Yes, ma'am!" Camila said with a salute while Gaby waved and stuck her tongue out at Carmen and me.

They will never grow up, and that's OK. Carmen and I are still pretty childish ourselves. There's a certain youthfulness to allowing our inner child to come out.

The girls were walking for a while when they noticed a vehicle driving slowly, parallel to them on the street. The high school they attended was a few blocks away, so they picked up their pace.

Luckily, the sun was still out. It was late, but the street was well-lit, and the fading sunlight allowed them to see the vehicle clearly.

---

[62] Mix of green plantains, ripe plantains, and yucca, with fried pork belly or fried pork rinds.

The windows were heavily tinted, impeding them from seeing the occupants.

"There they are," they heard a man's voice say as he lowered the window from the vehicle following them on the street. Gaby looked over nervously, recognizing his voice.

That's the stabber! Gaby thought, taking Camila's hand and running. She felt they needed to get away before the NYU assailant got out of the car.

"Hey, where do you two think you're going?" their pursuer yelled, exiting the car and chasing them.

You've got to be fucking kidding me, Camila thought, keeping up with Gaby. Just when they thought they would have an uneventful day … now this.

Let's take the shortcut between the houses to the school, Gaby thought, and Camila nodded.

"We're not going to be able to lose him. Someone else is following in the car. They'll take us if we don't vanish quickly," Camila yelled, running faster.

Let's teleport out of here! Gaby thought, yanking Camila's arm as she sped up.

"Think of Agent Jackson," Camila instructed as they turned into an alley between houses that led to the school.

"Are you out of your damn mind?" Gaby questioned, out of breath.

Camila took her hand. "Trust me. Quick, before he turns the corner and sees us disappear," she told Gaby.

"I don't think that's a good idea," Gaby protested. "Let's get back to Idely's and call the police," she pleaded.

"We don't have time for this, Gaby. Just think of Jackson, and let's get out of here!" Camila yelled as they turned into another back alley and continued to run toward the school.

"Fine, but I hope you know what you're doing," Gaby cautioned … and they vanished.

Their stalker turned the corner into the alley and sprinted but couldn't see them anywhere.

"Fuck!" he screamed in rage, clutching his head in frustration with both hands.

The girls popped up in Agent Jackson's living room. "Where are we?" Gaby asked, still shaken from the chase, clutching her chest as she gasped for air.

"I think we're at Jackson's house," Camila said breathlessly, looking around and seeing a picture of Jackson with an elderly woman on a shelf above an electric fireplace.

"Hands up!" Jackson ordered from the stairs and pointed a gun at them.

Camila and Gaby looked up at Agent Jackson and were so frightened by the sight of the weapon that they stood paralyzed with their hands in the air.

"What the hell are you two doing here?" Jackson demanded, agitated. "I could have shot you," she screamed, descending the rest of the stairs and holstering her gun.

The girls were still recovering from the shock of having a gun pointed at them and couldn't answer her straightaway. So, instead, they stood in the living room, squeezing each other's hands, and stared blankly at Jackson.

"Well, how did you get my address, and what are you doing here?" Jackson demanded angrily.

Funny how that works. Jackson can appear unannounced at *my* business looking for them, but they can't show up uninvited to *her* place without her throwing a fit.

"The maniac from NYU found us and was chasing us. We didn't know where else to go, so we came here. We found your address online," Gaby said after a moment.

"Online?" Jackson yelled. "I find that difficult to believe!" she stated, still staring at them incredulously.

"How did you get in?" Jackson continued to question as she walked toward the front door.

"Your door was unlocked when we got here, and we locked it when we came in, afraid he followed us. You have a gun, so we feel safe coming to you," Camila said, hoping to convince her.

"I doubt I left my front door unlocked!" Jackson countered as she examined the door.

"Dust it for prints then, but are you going to help us or not?

Someone just tried to kidnap us. Why don't you do *your* job and help us?" Gaby stressed.

"Didn't you say we could trust you?" Camila asked.

"Yes, I did, but none of this makes sense," Jackson admitted.

"It doesn't need to make sense. Just call it in. The men trying to kidnap us are probably still looking for us. Maybe they can be arrested or something," Gaby said wearily.

"Where were you being followed?" Jackson asked.

"Near our school," Camila answered.

"In Yonkers?" Jackson asked with heightened distrust.

"Where else?" Gaby asked sarcastically.

Gaby needed to slow down because Jackson was doing calculus with every word they uttered, and it was *not* looking good. We don't know where Jackson lives, get my drift?

"How long ago?" Jackson quizzed.

"Um, I'm not sure, maybe twenty minutes ago," Camila said nervously.

I'm about to choke on my popcorn over here. I don't know why Camila thought it was a good idea to go to Jackson in the first place. They could've just thought of going to the nearest police station. Of course, that psycho would be in handcuffs by now, but instead, they are in Jackson's place, and their math is just not adding up to her, but let us carry on.

"How did you get here?" Jackson asked them as she sat on her royal blue chaise. She just turned the FBI agent all the way up, if you know what I mean.

Where is here? Where are we? Gaby thought, unsure, and Camila shrugged her shoulders.

See, I told you we shouldn't come here, Gaby complained in her thoughts, and Camila gently shook her head.

Now, they're in a world of shit because Camila did not think this through, and she acted on impulse.

I try to teach them to think before they act and to attempt to have all the facts before doing anything. Jackson is an intelligent woman. Fooling her will be nigh on impossible.

"Cat got your tongue, or have you ladies run out of lies?" Jackson continued the interrogation.

"That's the thing with lies," she continued before the girls could answer. I feel she knows they cannot reply without giving themselves up.

"Once you say one lie, you have to say another, and then another, until the charade falls apart," Jackson continued, and the girls stood silently.

Jackson's home was immaculately clean. The living room was small but furnished in good taste, with the chaise, a matching love seat, and an exotic Delco abstract art coffee table in the center.

Unfortunately, she had no television, only two striking Kalimera feather floor lamps, and an electric fireplace against the wall.

Everything seemed expensive and color-coordinated. For example, the feathers on the lamps were also royal blue with gold legs.

"I'm sorry we came here. Going to the police would've been a better idea, but since you seem so bothered and are keeping illegal tabs on us, we thought you would jump at the opportunity to help, but I see that you don't care. You're just nosy and desperate to be right about us hiding something," Gaby told her accusatorially.

My girl is trying to flip the script. I'll admit she's good, but I'm not sure that'll be enough to get them out of this mess.

"You think you can break into my home and disrespect me, young lady?" Jackson asked, sitting upright.

I would insert some emojis for emphasis, but I don't think that's allowed in storytelling. So let's see what happens.

"We didn't break into your house, and she means no disrespect," Camila replied defensively.

Not looking like such a good idea now, is it? But no matter how much advise you try to give a person, there is no better teacher than experience.

"I'm sorry if you were offended, but the truth often has that effect. We're leaving. You'll continue to accuse us of something anyway instead of helping. If you're not going to help catch the homicidal maniac after us, please leave us alone," Gaby said, ushering Camila to the door.

These two were testing this woman's patience. I hope she doesn't call in a break-in and have them both arrested. But yes, she should have them arrested, which may teach them a lesson.

Camila is stubborn when she thinks she's right. Unfortunately, this "seeing the good in people" will probably land her in jail tonight.

"Not so fast. You two are not going to 'bamboozle' me with nonsense. You still haven't told me how you got here, and I'm still not convinced you didn't break-in. So I want answers, and I want them *now*," Agent Jackson demanded as she stood to her feet.

"You want answers?" Camila shouted, strained.

Oh boy, please don't. Don't do it, girl. For the love of God, don't!

"Camila, please, don't," Gaby pleaded, looking her directly in the eyes.

It's OK! Camila said to Gaby without verbalizing.

She turned to Jackson, "If you want answers, I suggest you first sit," she recommended.

Agent Jackson sat again with a disturbed look, and Gaby joined her partner in crime on the love seat, bracing for impact.

"We have supernatural powers, we are telepathic, and we can teleport," Camila blurted out.

If you've ever had a Brazilian wax, you know that fast is the best way to rip that wax off, and Camila just jumped right to it with no preliminaries.

Meanwhile, Jackson sat there trying to process what she just said.

I bet she's debating between Camila being crazy or joking, but who knows what her reaction will be? I only hope Camila knows what she's doing because there is no going back from this.

We are masters of our silence and prisoners of our words. Once they are said, we cannot take them back. Therefore, it is wise to consider what we say carefully because the impact is often insufferable. The heat of the moment has caused more regret than anything else in this world.

EPISODE ELEVEN

Thiago and Paulo cut their weekend trip short because they insisted on returning tonight instead of Sunday night as planned. They had been calling the girls, but no one answered.

Thiago was worried something awful had happened, and Paulo could feel his restlessness. It must be the twin connection. They communicate without the need for words, not supernaturally as the girls do, but there is a special connection between them.

"Let's call Idelfonsa. Camila and Gabriela are probably still there," Paulo suggested, seeing that Thiago was distraught.

Paulo doesn't like sensing that Thiago is sad or upset. When they were kids, he always tried making funny faces and doing unusual stunts like hanging from the railing on the stairs to cheer up his brother.

If that's not unconditional love, I don't know what is. Paulo is entertaining because he's been practicing since childhood for the role.

"Yeah, I'll give her a call," Thiago said miserably, reaching for his phone.

My phone rang. It was Thiago.

"How are you, Idelfonsa? Are Camila and Gabriela there?" he asked me.

"I'm well. How was the trip? Did you boys like the campus?" I asked.

"It was all right. I have no complaints. So, are the girls there?" he asked again.

"Oh no, they left over an hour ago."

"Seriously? Because we've been trying to get in touch with them with no luck," he said agonizingly.

I told him they walked, so they're probably still on their way … although they should've been home by now.

Now, I'm scared. I told the girls to call as soon as they got home, and I still haven't heard from them.

Of course, they could've taken a slow walk and possibly stopped for ice cream, but I'm starting to get a bad feeling. Well, with all that's happened, I'm constantly worried.

Thiago told me he'd drive around their regular route to see if he could spot them, and I told him that was a good idea.

"Keep me informed, and as soon as you hear from them, please let me know," I said before ending the call.

"What's with the grave face?" Carmen asked.

"It was Thiago. He says they're back and haven't been able to contact Camila or Gabriel. He seems worried, so now *I'm* concerned. They left over an hour ago. They should've already been home," I said hysterically.

"It's a beautiful summer night. They probably stopped somewhere, and their phones are silent or dead, so relax," she laughed.

Thiago drove through his neighborhood with the car windows lowered, and all his senses heightened.

Many were sitting on the front porch enjoying a beer, and children played outside, so he drove cautiously.

The sky was clear, and the moon was full. Thiago heard music faintly playing as he drove by a house that seemed to be hosting a party.

He was now near the high school. He slowed down, knowing that if they were walking home, they'd take the shortcut he and Paulo showed them, but there was no sign of the girls anywhere.

Dejected, he raised the car windows, turned on the air-conditioning, and drove off.

"They probably teleported somewhere cool. Camila and Gaby will be back soon. You'll see," Paulo guaranteed Thiago.

What if they teleported somewhere and didn't tell me, afraid I'd object? I hope they haven't gotten themselves into any trouble, I thought, standing by the kitchen counter with Midnight by my side.

"I only care that they're safe. But you know, it's unlike the girls not to answer their phones or tell anyone where they are. So if they didn't want to tell us, fine, but they could've told Idelfonsa. She's been worried sick these last couple of weeks," Thiago added sadly.

These episodes were getting out of control. I've never suffered from anxiety and now find myself constantly on edge. I need Camila and Gabriela to turn up soon.

Suddenly, the doorbell rang, and I rushed downstairs. It was unusual for anyone to visit this late in the evening.

"Hey, Idelfonsa," Thiago said as I let him and Paulo enter.

Paulo nodded a half smile, and I looked outside down the street, hoping to see the girls before locking the door.

"Any luck?" I asked, already knowing the answer. It was a hopeful impromptu question.

"Nope, we didn't see them anywhere," Paulo said as Thiago shook his head.

"Did they say anything before they left?" Thiago asked, deeply troubled.

I shook my head. I already went over the details when he called earlier. He must think I left out the specifics, but I told him everything exactly as it happened. He's just overly preoccupied, and I can relate.

"Come up. I'll make some tea, and we can wait to hear from the girls together. Should we call their house?" I asked, unsure, as they followed me upstairs.

"I called Gaby's house, and her mother told me she hadn't been home all day and to try her cell," Paulo informed me.

"I wonder where they could be," I said as Carmen joined us in the kitchen.

"Any word?" she asked, sitting at the dining table with the rest of us.

I have a large eat-in kitchen/dining space. When I was a kid, my parents converted the actual dining room into a guest room, but this kitchen is so big that we can still fit another table in.

I felt my phone buzz in my pocket and fumbled it as I retrieved it when I saw it was a text from Gaby.

You're not going to freaking believe this! it read.

I bit my nails in anguish because that's all she wrote, and the anticipation was excruciating.

"What is it?" Carmen asked, seeing the expression on my face.

"It's Gaby. She—" I couldn't complete the sentence because as soon as I mentioned Gaby's name, Thiago and Paulo jumped out of their seats and snatched the phone from my hand.

"What did she say? Where are they?" Thiago desperately asked as Paulo looked over his shoulder at my phone in his hands.

"Why don't you just read for yourself since you're so eager," I told him, annoyed.

"That's it!" Thiago said, reading the text.

"It doesn't say anything, really," Paulo said, shrugging his shoulders and handing the phone back to me.

"I know, Sherlock. You'd know if you would've allowed me to finish what I was going to say," I barked.

Midnight jumped on my lap and purred against my chest. The cat must be telling me to calm down. What Midnight doesn't know is that her little friends Camila and Gabriela will be the death of me.

"Is someone going to tell me what Gaby said, or do I have to read it myself?" Carmen asked as she looked at the boys and me.

She would have to read it herself, so I handed her my phone. "I bet we won't believe it!" Carmen said with a chuckle after reading Gaby's text.

Like Gaby, she found humor in everything. While the boys and I were losing our minds, she was amused. I gave her a nasty look, telling her I didn't think any of this was funny.

"What? You all need to relax. That text is a good sign, and I bet something ridiculous follows it. She could've written to call the police. *That* would've been scary, but that lets me know they're okay," she assured us.

I rolled my eyes, knowing she was right. I guess what's irritating is that I didn't get more information. What did they get into that will be so shocking to the rest of us?

Carmen made chamomile tea to ease our nerves, and we waited for Gaby to send more information about their whereabouts.

"We're at Agent Jackson's!" Gaby wrote with *six* exclamation points. !!!!!!

"If this girl doesn't hurry up and tell me exactly what's happening, I will smash this phone against the wall. It's like needing morphine after surgery and getting it one drip at a time from a slow IV," I yelled in frustration.

What's killing me is that they're at Agent Jackson's, and what exactly does that mean "at Agent Jackson's"? Office? Home? And like why?

Why on earth are they with that woman? This situation is too much. I wanted to strangle Camila because Gaby couldn't stand Jackson. So I'm convinced this was Camila's idea.

"What is it?" Carmen asked.

"She was right. You won't believe this. They're with Jackson," I informed everyone.

Of course, they were throwing darts at me with their looks, and I knew what it was like to experience unnecessary confusion with the lack of information, so I quickly told them I didn't know anything else.

"Wait—Jackson, as in the FBI agent?" Paulo asked disbelievingly.

Carmen has turned scarlet and is pugnaciously shaking her head and fists. I hope she doesn't have an aneurysm.

"*Ésa misma!*"[63] I said, and the boys looked at me perplexed because they don't speak Spanish.

There's no need to translate because Carmen erupts, confirming it is *The* Agent Jackson.

"How could they? Why would they go to her and not come here to us if something happened? Because the only logical explanation for them to be there is that something happened," Carmen shouted, outraged.

I was about to attempt to calm Carmen when *poof*, Camila and Gaby were standing in our midst, and Thiago soared out of his seat and nuzzled Camila tightly against his chest.

"Where were you?" Paulo asked Gaby, pulling her into him around her waist.

Smiling, she kissed him and gently bit his lower lip. "Were you afraid for my life, baby?" Gaby asked him drolly.

"Yes, silly. What is all that about being with the FBI agent?" he probed.

Gaby skipped around the kitchen whimsically, flapping her arms. "Oh, it was indeed an epic adventure. First, we almost got kidnapped,

---

[63] The same one.

and then Camila decided we should go to Agent Jackson instead of coming here, and I'm sure she'd be delighted to tell you all the rest!" Gaby finished, standing still and derisively staring at Camila.

We looked from Camila to Gaby, sensing animosity. Finally, we gawped at Camila, hoping she would elaborate.

Disheartened, Camila escaped Thiago's hold and sat. "You're so damn theatrical, Gaby. You should join the circus," Camila said condescendingly.

"And you're selfish, only thinking about yourself, going on your stupid whim and exposing us to Jackson!" Gaby roared at Camila, infuriated.

"What?" I shrieked, standing and hovering over Camila, awaiting her account.

Camila looked down at her hands and inhaled deeply. "I thought we would be safe if we went to her. I was afraid coming here would endanger the rest of you, and I desperately wanted her to take some action to have that creep following us arrested," Camila said, and no one spoke, so she continued.

"Jackson was more concerned with how we got into her house and drilled us about it until there was nothing left to say. I know she would've had us arrested for trespassing if she wasn't satisfied we were being frank, so I told her the truth," Camila concluded—and we gasped. Gaby still looked at her with antipathy.

"Wow, babe, that's crazy. Why would you trust her?" Thiago asked, reaching for her hand.

Camila took her hand away and placed them under her thighs. Thiago looked bruised but didn't say anything.

"What did she say?" Carmen asked, which was what we were all thinking but dumbfounded to articulate.

"This is the *best* part," said Gaby darkly before Camila could respond.

Camila looked at Gaby apologetically. "She said I was a lying sack of shit, so I took Gaby's hand and came here and left her to figure it out," Camila said with a lump in her throat and abruptly hurdled out of the chair and ran out of the kitchen into the botanica and out to the street.

Thiago frantically raced after her while Carmen and I stared at each other with mouths agape. Gaby had a fixed smirk on her face that I couldn't read, and Paulo was as surprised as we were.

"What would possess her to tell her the truth and then prove it by teleporting in front of her?" Carmen asked bombastically.

I couldn't speak yet. I was still astonished by Camila's naivety. I needed to fix this, and I needed to employ damage control quickly. It was only a matter of time before Jackson showed up, demanding answers, and I better have a remarkable story for her.

Right now, I feel the girls' relationship might need some mending. Sometimes, the injury is so severe that we can never fully recover and get things back to how they once were, but their love is strong. They'll overcome this.

"Don't you think you were unfairly harsh on her, Gaby? She thought she was doing the right thing," I said.

"Unbelievable. *She* fucks up, and *I* get chastised for it, but I'm not surprised. She can never do any wrong, and I can never get anything right. Screw you, Idelfonsa. Screw you! Your precious baby is an idiot, and if you're sad she has her feelings hurt over her stupidity, don't take it out on me," she yelled and stormed out.

"Um, thanks for everything. You know, Gaby doesn't mean that. When things with Cam aren't right, she gets—"

I interrupted Paulo. "Tensions are high, and apologies to me are needless," I said.

He nodded awkwardly, unsure what else to say, and I was surprised he was still standing there.

"It's OK. None of this is Gaby's fault. I know that. It's just that I don't want anything coming between her and Camila. Go after her and make sure she's OK," I said, and he darted off.

"Hey, wait up," Paulo said to Gaby before she could make it out the door.

She stopped holding the door open with a foot and snarkily told him to hurry up.

"Idelfonsa only wants you and Camila to be good. So you didn't have to be rude," he said, catching up with her at the door. Immediately, Gaby took her foot off it, allowing it to slam in his face.

"Since my feelings mean nothing to you too, screw *you*, Paulo," she said and walked away.

Paulo ran after her and grabbed her hand. "Oh, come on, not me too. I'm sorry. I know you're upset, and I'm on your side. I only tell you this because I love you. Come on, let me take you home," he said, pulling her toward his car.

Silently she followed him and got in as he opened the door. You know he does not want any problems with Gaby when opening the car door for her.

"Where are Camila and Thiago anyway?" he asked.

"Who cares? Let's go," Gaby said indifferently but looked out the window as Paulo drove off for signs of them.

"Camila, let's go back to the car so I can take you home. It's midnight. It would be best if you were home as soon as possible," Thiago pleaded as Camila walked faster, tears streaming down her face.

"Thiago, just leave me alone," she said, wiping her nose.

"I'll leave you alone as soon as you are home safe, so stop being stubborn and get back to the car. This behavior is why you got into this disaster in the first place," he said, provoking her.

Camila turned to face him, enraged. "Fuck you, Thiago. Fuck all of you! I didn't ask for this. I didn't want to 'tele-fucking-port!' Gaby was the one pushing this shit, and I'm tired of everyone expecting *me* to be perfect. I hope Jackson takes me to some freaking lab, and I don't have to see any of you again," she yelled, walking away again.

"Hey! Hey, wait up. No one is expecting you to be anything but yourself. None of this is anyone's fault, so calm down. Let me take you home, then you can do whatever you want," he begged.

"No, and let me take this opportunity to tell you something I've meant to say. It's over. Go to MIT, a single man, and enjoy the rest of your life. Leave me alone," she said coldly, running away.

Remember that heat-of-the-moment comment I made before? Well, insert that statement here.

It had been drizzling spasmodically, and now, the skies opened with torrential rain. Thiago stood there watching her fade away as his world came crashing down with the heavy shower.

"Thiago, Thiago, Thiago," Paulo screamed from the car but had to get out and shake him.

"Bro, what the fuck? You're getting soaked. Come on, get in," he said, towing him inside the car.

Thiago was comatose but managed to say, "Find Camila. She ran off."

Gaby quivered with terror as guilt enveloped her in a tight grip. "What happened?" she cried out, but Thiago was unresponsive.

"Fuck fuck fuck," Gaby screamed, banging on the dash.

Paulo drove slowly, hoping to find Camila. He went around a few times but didn't see her. "Call her in your head," he told Gaby, who rolled her eyes without response.

We all know Camila's not going to answer Gaby. I don't think she wants anything to do with us right now. It's easy to want to find blame with someone, but I think we're all to blame here. Maybe the one we're mad at is the only one who is right, and the truth will somehow set us all free.

"She's probably already home, and I have zero visibility, so I'll take you home, Gaby. There's no point in aimlessly driving around in this storm."

Gaby nodded as fresh tears rolled down her face.

I was restless and couldn't sleep, so I sat up to see Midnight admiring the rainstorm from the window. It started as a beautiful day with clear skies, and the moon was bright and high in the sky when they left. It's as if Mother Nature was grieving for them, as though their mood affects the weather.

"I wish I hadn't said that to Gaby," I told myself.

I hoped we could get past this and return to how things were.

"That bitch," I thought of Jackson.

Although I wanted to blame someone, my anger was misplaced. It was my fault. *I'm* the adult in this equation. I should've handled this responsibly by telling Gaby's and Camila's parents. The girls were in danger, and I've been negligent.

EPISODE TWELVE

A couple of weeks passed, and I hadn't heard from or seen the kids. Carmen had been moping around, and even Midnight appeared gloomy. I missed them and hoped they found a way to patch up things.

Thiago's roots have withered and dried, like a bare tree, without Camila. He rarely left his room, and when he did, he sulked and snapped at anyone who attempted to speak with him.

He's not communicative, and Paulo was worried. They were packing for MIT, and Paulo wondered if Thiago would go to Camila's to say goodbye but was afraid to ask.

Thiago had sunk into a deep depression. Not only was he sad, but also overcome by resentment fluctuating between love and hate. He was angry with Camila, speculating how she could have been so cruel to end it that way.

"I didn't deserve this shit," he mumbled as he threw some belongings into a box. *I devoted my entire life to her, and* this *is how she repays me?* he thought, fighting tears.

"I wish I never met her!" he shouted to his empty room, tears now rushing down his face.

I was dreading this day. I respected Camila's decision, but she could've just let the relationship fade into oblivion with the distance so this pain could've been minimized.

I won't say "avoided" because their breakup was bound to be painful despite the how, but this bitterness he now felt tarnishes all the beautiful memories they once shared.

Although some resentment always accompanied even the friendliest of breakups, I prayed Thiago could get past this and recover some of his friendship with Camila some day.

I'm confident that Camila's intentions were never to hurt him but to set him free and liberate herself.

It gets complicated trying to find oneself while navigating a relationship. Maybe Camila felt trapped. She was trying to figure out a lot at home. With the upcoming shifts in her life, the relationship was too much to handle emotionally.

Relationships are attachments between people; when one person severs ties, there's trauma, and both suffer. That is the inevitable truth.

Emotional maturity is learning to accept things for what they are and letting go with gratitude, but that is something we know as we grow through our life experiences.

I know there is nothing to forgive, but I hope Thiago can pardon Camila for hurting him and unburden himself from the awful resentment he now feels.

Camila has been in her room for weeks, and her mother is oblivious to her despair. However, she is happy to spend more time with Camila at home, even if she is tucked away in her room. The only thing she finds odd is Camila's lack of appetite.

Camila cries herself to sleep every night. She lost the love of her life and her best friend too. She experiences a deep sadness that leaks into her soul's bottomless, murkiest crevasses, leaving her to feel empty and despairing.

The days have lost their color, and Camila feels lost in a gray fog that seems to envelop the entire city. Time passes slowly, and her chest feels heavy as if her heart were sinking into a dark abyss.

A hopeless sensation of drowning from the inside out consumes her, and she prefers to sleep to avoid confronting the intolerable pain devouring her.

Finally, after weeks of isolation, her mother confronts her and asks what's happening. "*¿Por qué no estás comiendo?*"[64] she asked Camila.

Camila exploded, "Leave me alone!" she cried and stormed out of the house, rushing downstairs, tripping but catching herself on the railing before she could fall.

---

[64] Why aren't you eating?

Her mother watched aghast and was deeply troubled by Camila's bizarre behavior.

Camila slammed her front door and saw Paulo and Gaby sitting on Gaby's front steps.

"Hey, Camila," Paulo said.

Camila looked over and waved awkwardly before running away.

"What's up with her?" Paulo asked Gaby.

"I don't know. That's the first time I've seen Camila in weeks," she said, still staring in the direction she fled.

She won't admit it, but Gaby desperately misses her, yet she won't make the first move to get her back.

Haughtiness often prevents us from fixing meaningful relationships. We shouldn't just walk away from the people we care about because we have differences or things get complicated. Instead, we need to fight for what we love.

Mama Bear found her phone and urgently looked for her husband's number through the contacts. "*Amor*,[65] I think our daughter is taking drugs," she told him in a panicked voice.

"My love, I doubt Camila is on drugs, but I'll talk to her later, OK?" he said calmly.

Camila made her way to Central Park. Near the 100th Street entrance was a beautiful body of water known as The Pool. She lay on the lawn, attempting to see the beauty of this place as she once did but was overwhelmed by thoughts of Thiago.

The serene landscape is a lush scenic view of beautiful red maples, sweetgums, willows, and wildlife. The willows are Camila's favorite. The fall foliage is gorgeous, but she loves the greenery of summer.

She and Thiago would visit this place for romantic picnics and discuss spending the rest of their lives together. Those were simpler times when their grades were their only worry.

Fresh tears sneaked out of her eyes, rolling until the grass received them, and they seeped into the earth sacramentally.

Ironic how you can shed your bluest tears in the place that brought you the purest joy.

---

[65] Beloved!

"Thiago isn't doing well," Paulo told Gaby as she stretched her legs across his, still sitting on her front steps.

"Of course! We all knew that it would be devastating when that relationship came to an end. She's probably losing her shit too. She loves him. I know she broke up with him because she's afraid he'll forget her once he goes to MIT and starts to meet hot, intellectual chicks," Gaby said.

"That's crazy. Camila is brilliant!" Paulo protested.

"I know, but she wasn't going to be able to handle a heartbreak of that scale, so she broke her own heart," Gaby said sadly.

"We're going to be together forever, baby!" Paulo said as he kissed Gaby on the cheek.

"I love your sweet lies, handsome," she said, her lips interlocked with his.

I hate making comparisons, but that could've been Camila. But she likes to overanalyze and be extra intense for no reason.

Life is easy. We, humans, insist on making it complicated. We are addicted to suffering and frequently sabotage our own happiness.

"You think the girls patched things up already?" Carmen asked as we stacked some new books.

"I don't know, but I sure hope so."

"Any chance we'll see them again?" she asked, handing me a book about blocked chakras.

"I'm sure we will, Nena. But we need to give them time," I told her confidently.

Time heals all wounds. I know we will all be together again and laugh, recalling how Camila thought it would be a good idea to confide in Jackson.

"I hope so." Carmen acknowledged that the girls gave her life. "I love having them around," she said.

"That makes two of us," I told her mournfully, and Midnight circled my feet, pressing her cheeks on my legs.

I felt I had a purpose with those kids in my life. They've been coming around for four years. I've been a part of their life for these crucial years, and I've seen them grow into amazing men and women. It will shatter my heart to pieces, never to see them again.

Fortunately, the business has been busy. So, Carmen and I have been focusing on managing the new web page to keep our minds off the girls.

One morning soon after opening, I heard the door jingle, and I jumped, looking over excitedly. I only know of two people who come in this early.

"Expecting someone else?" she asked, reading the disappointment on my face.

Carmen looked at me and shook her head. It's way too early for this. We don't have the energy to deal with any nonsense right now.

"To what do I owe this early visit?" I asked Agent Jackson as she reached me.

"You're going to play coy?" she said, smiling at us like we were besties.

"It's too early for games," I said, already irritated.

"Where are the super friends?" she asks, looking around.

"The super who?" I inquired, playing the fool.

I will not admit to anything until I speak with the girls, and if that's never, I'll take their abilities to the grave. I will give Jackson nothing.

"I have good news," Jackson announced with excitement.

She knew she needed to get straight to the point because I'm too grown to fall for her FBI Jedi mind tricks.

"What's that?" I asked doubtfully.

"I pulled some strings with your local police and obtained surveillance footage depicting the creep stalking the girls. As a result, the car's plate number returned to a sketchy individual who was arrested and sang like a bird," she happily told Carmen and me.

Now, she's trying to pull our heartstrings with this *I'm on your side. I'm trying to help* stunt—no, lady, you're just doing your job. She's a one-person show playing good cop/bad cop all by herself.

"And?" I asked, unimpressed, as she made herself comfortable on one of the stools by the counter.

"Thanks to the snitch, we arrested the freak. He's in custody as we speak," she declared triumphantly and crossed her legs, revealing some fancy platform sandals under her long summer dress.

"Finally, you did some actual work," Carmen said feebly.

Jackson ignored her, and after a few minutes of silent observation, she walked over to the bookshelves. I think she was hoping the girls would run downstairs like in the past.

"Anything on telepathy?" she queried, reading the titles.

Now, she's pressing my buttons. She's got some freaking nerve. She has turned our lives upside down with her intrusion.

"I sell books for spirituality, not fantasy," I said coldly.

"You and I both know it's no fantasy," she said, looking at me.

I held the stare, and honestly, if I could punch her in the face, I would. I've never felt so angry before.

Yeah, I'm projecting my anger. It probably has nothing to do with her, but it makes me feel better.

"I don't understand what you mean, but is there a point to your visit?" I asked.

She sneered, and I fought the urge to heave the book I held at her head.

"As a matter of fact, there is. I need Camila and Gabriela to testify," she said, pulling out a book, *Becoming Supernatural*, turning it over to read its description.

"Well, why are you telling me? I'm not responsible for them," I said, visibly irked.

"Why so touchy? I thought you'd be delighted with the news," she said inquiringly.

"I just feel *you* should let them know," I said defensively.

"I assumed this was the best place to find them since they're always here, but I see there's trouble in paradise," she said, getting on my nerves.

Carmen let out a loud sigh and made her hands into fists.

"You know what they say about assumptions, right?" I asked scornfully.

I don't dislike Agent Jackson, and I feel she doesn't dislike us, either. We are just on the opposing sides of the aisle. I don't think she means the girls any harm, but she doesn't understand the damage her insistence can and has caused.

"Don't worry. I'll make proper notifications for Ms. De Los Santos and Ms. Hernandez, Ms. Perez. May I call you Idelfonsa?" she asked, and I thought she was being genuine for once.

"Call me whatever you fancy," I replied, and she smiled.

"I only hope you can make the trial, which will be fascinating, with Gaby being so litigious," she said poignantly.

"There will be no trial. That lunatic will take a plea," I promised Jackson, as my Orisha is my witness.

She laughed loudly, and I was unsure what she found so amusing, but I didn't care enough to ask, so I gave her a solemn stare.

"It's always a pleasure, ladies. We can address the elephant in the room when the gang is back together. So, ciao for now," she said, putting on her sunglasses and heading for the door.

"The pleasure is seeing you out. Sayonara," Carmen muttered behind her.

Agent Jackson waved without turning, violently shaking her hips as she went.

I want to say I hope I never see her again, but I feel that's not the last any of us will see of Agent Jackson.

She's like that pebble in your shoe that you can't get out, the thorn in your side, the annoying neighbor … Well, you get it.

My only concern now is this trial. I don't know how Jackson will let the girls know, but I hope the girls' parents are made aware. On another note, let's see what's going on over there.

The boys are having a farewell party. Gaby had an impulse to go over and ask Camila to come with her but changed her mind before she could make it up her front steps and quickly got in the taxi waiting for her.

I'd love to say it's the party of the century, but it's not. Instead, it's a small gathering with the twins' family and close friends. So, it's only Gaby, their soccer coach, and João, a boy on the team attending MIT.

I declined the invitation. I didn't know if my presence would upset Gaby. So, I told Carmen to go without me. Their beef is with me, I told her.

The boys were their own best friends, so they had a small circle like Gaby and Camila. Thiago was beside himself with Camila not attending and didn't say much. Gaby could see the pain on his face and wished she would've dragged Camila along.

The boys' parents decorated the house nicely with balloons and congratulations banners and had a cake for them. *Good Luck*, it read.

Gaby wore a short, black, strapless dress that hugged all the curves in the right places. Her lips were a bright red lipstick, and she wore black leather Converse sneakers.

"You look gorgeous," Paulo whispered, and she smiled, lighting up the room.

"Thanks, my love," she told him with a kiss.

"God, my heart aches for Thiago. He didn't deserve this. She could've at least shown up to say goodbye. They weren't just dating. She was his closest friend. That was cold," Paulo said to Gaby as he caressed her arm.

"This goodbye would've devastated her. So she played it her way in the end, easing the pain. Don't bear a grudge against her. She's also aching over their breakup, I know it," Gaby revealed.

"That's the crazy thing. It doesn't have to be goodbye. We aren't moving to Brazil. We're only going to be a few hours away, and you guys can go wherever you want instantly. So I don't get what this whole production is about," Paulo said, baffled.

I agreed with Paulo. However, this is not for us to understand *cada cabeza es un mundo*.[66] We all deal with situations differently and shouldn't judge anyone who does things contrary to us.

"Everyone has their way of coping. I know it may appear messed up, but I understand her. I believe that someday, Thiago and Camila will be friends again. True love never dies. It simply evolves. She taught me that," Gaby replied emotionally, thinking of Camila.

Gaby is correct. Our girl is resilient and will emerge wiser and stronger from this experience, and so will Thiago.

But deep down, Gaby felt anger because Paulo was right. Because of their unique ability, the boys being away meant nothing to Camila and Gaby. However, Gaby will always stick up for Camila.

Since the boys were off early the following day, Gaby spent the night so that she could see Paulo off. She had breakfast with the boys in the morning and helped them load the car.

"You better not cheat on me, or I'll make you regret it," Gaby warned Paulo.

---

[66] Each head is a world.

Paulo laughed. "Yeah, because boys are the only ones who cheat, right?" he said to her.

"I'm a saint. Can't say the same about those trashy girls that dorm in school, though, so if you lose me, it'll be your loss," Gaby replied, winking at him.

"I know, babe. You have nothing to worry about," he promised her.

"Be good, you two," she said to them after Paulo gave her a long kiss and embrace. Then they got into the car.

Gaby felt her chest tighten, and a knot formed in her throat. She didn't think she would cry, but a silent tear rolled down her cheek, and at that moment, she longed for Camila.

"See you later, alligator," Paulo said, waving, but she could not manage to speak. So instead, she contorted her face with a smile and returned the wave.

Mr. and Mrs. Silva also stood outside, waving goodbye with radiantly proud smiles.

"Stay for lunch, Gabriela," Paulo's mother said, and Gaby nodded, following them inside.

Mr. and Mrs. Silva dropped Gaby off in the afternoon just as Camila was heading out, and Mrs. Silva immediately got out of the car.

"Hey, Camila, we missed you yesterday," she said as she caught up with Camila outside her house.

Camila gave her a sheepish half smile and shrugged her shoulders.

"How are you holding up, honey?" she asked Camila, who collapsed into her arms, weeping.

Mrs. Silva held her tightly and tried to console her while she cried, and Gaby rushed inside her house, unable to witness it.

"It's going to be OK, I promise you, and just so you know, Thiago is lost without you. I've never seen him hurt so much before in his life. So, please, reach out and save your friendship; I'm begging you," she told Camila.

Camila wiped her face but could not utter a word. "Come by sometime. I'll make your favorite," Mrs. Silva promised as she got back into the car.

"Okay," Camila managed to say almost inaudibly.

Camila watched as they turned the corner and disappeared, then another vehicle parked in front of her house.

"Just the girl I wanted to see," Jackson said, exiting the car.

Gaby had been peering out the window, and seeing Jackson, she immediately ran out of the house.

"Now, it's a party," Jackson said, delighted when she saw Gaby.

"What do you want, lady?" a belligerent Gaby asked.

"I have fantastic news for both of you," she said, beaming.

As things weren't already good, they got better as the plot thickened when Camila's mom walked outside.

She peeped at everything from the window, so she witnessed the whole scene with Thiago's mother, but it killed her since she didn't know who Jackson was.

"*¿Camila, quien es esa mujer?*"[67] she asked as soon as the door opened.

Camila felt a pit form in her stomach. "*Tierra tragame!*"[68] she thought, wishing to disappear, and Gaby regretted having come outside.

That Spanish flows when shit gets real.

"Is this your mother, Camila?" Jackson asked, walking up the stairs.

I have to admit I'm ecstatic that this is about to happen. Keeping this type of secret from parents is wrong.

I know it's not my place to divulge it, but I will reiterate what Carmen said: keeping this secret is dangerous, so I hope Jackson spills all the tea.

---

[67]   Camila, who is that woman?
[68]   Earth swallow me!

EPISODE THIRTEEN

The boys settled in their dorm room. Paulo was excited and looking forward to learning about the campus and making new friends. Although he enjoyed high school and his life back home, there is much more he wants to do and experience.

Thiago is apathetic. He has no interest in going anywhere. He already acquired most of his textbooks in a failed attempt to distract himself from the breakup with Camila. While Paulo is around, he reads his books.

He doesn't want Paulo to keep attempting to get him to talk about it. There was nothing to say. Camila dumped him, and he feels like shit. The end. And if reading every textbook is going to take his mind off it, so be it.

However, if he keeps that up, he will be the one to teach his classes. At least Thiago is channeling his energy productively. When Paulo told him he would meet many new girls, he got angry and said girls are a stupid distraction.

The positive side of this is that Thiago will finish top of his class because his only concern right now is his career. So, perhaps this was a blessing in disguise. Maybe this was what he needed to do his best and not worry about Camila.

I believe that everything happens for a reason and usually for our highest good, even if initially it doesn't appear that way.

He may say that girls are a distraction, but soon, he will meet someone else, and even though he may not forget Camila completely, it will no longer bother him that they are not together. He might even be glad one day.

Their room is small. It has two twin beds and two desks, nothing they aren't already used to except that Thiago had the privacy of his own room at home.

"Weren't the boys leaving today?" Carmen asked after we had breakfast. Camila got her into eating mangú con los tres golpes,[69] so now she makes it all the time.

So much for eating light in the mornings. Those girls are a terrible influence.

"Oh yeah, they sent a text saying goodbye, sent us all their love, said they were a little behind schedule and couldn't stop by this morning before leaving," I told Carmen as I got up from the dining table.

"Did they say anything about the girls?" she asked, hopeful, sipping her café con leche.[70]

"Paulo said they were sad we didn't make it last night and mentioned Gaby had spent the night so she could help them pack the car in the morning, but no mention of Camila. But they did promise to visit soon," I said, cleaning up the table and placing the dirty dishes in the sink.

"Ah, Camila didn't show up. That must've crushed Thiago, but I'm sure she had her reasons. I wish we would've gone," she said sadly, joining me at the sink to help me wash the dishes.

"I told you to go. I didn't want to make it awkward with Gaby being mad at me," I reminded her as I dried a plate.

"No, comai, I wasn't going to go without you. It's all right. The boys will be back before we know it," she said, smiling.

I returned the smile, amused that if we were experiencing an empty nest, I could not imagine what their parents were going through. Then I laughed, presuming they were thrilled. We only got the kids in small doses. They were stuck with them all this time.

"*El que solo se ríe de su picardía se acuerda,*"[71] Carmen said, and we giggled.

---

[69] Mashed green plantains, fried salami, fried eggs, fried cheese, with red onion garnish.
[70] Coffee with milk.
[71] He who laughs to himself recalls his mischief.

Meanwhile, Camila has a situation to handle. She is grieving and now must deal with Jackson coming unannounced to her house.

"Agent Jackson, I'm right here. No need to enter my home. If you have something you'd like to discuss, I suggest you do so with me. I'm an adult," Camila said, peeved before Jackson could reach her mother.

Mrs. De Los Santos wanted to interject, but she's never before witnessed Camila speak so firmly, and after seeing her with Thiago's mother, she opted to remain silent.

"I'll be right in, Mom. Wait inside," she said, and Mama Bear acknowledged this and went into the house, feeling a sense of pride seeing Camila command with authority.

I presume that she worries about Camila's gentle and passive demeanor. She probably thinks she will be a pushover, but that is far from true. It is a mistake to confuse kindness with weakness.

Gaby skipped over to stand beside Camila. No matter what, that's her ride or die, even if she goes back to giving her the silent treatment.

"My, you're spicy today," Jackson said with a grin, but Camila was not amused.

"Let me clarify, Agent Jackson, don't ever come to my home unexpectedly unless you have a warrant. I suggest you find another way to contact me in the future," Camila advised her commandingly.

"Understood, but what is going on with the gang? You're all in foul moods," she said, removing the sunglasses she wore and further exasperating Camila.

"Why are you here?" Gaby asked, knowing Camila was a ticking time bomb.

"I have good news," Jackson told them.

Meanwhile, Camila's mother stood by the window anxiously waiting to know who this mysterious woman was.

Camila called her "agent." Of what? Is she an official? Is Camila in trouble? she questioned as she looked on.

"What?" Camila asked shortly.

"The creep stalking you ladies is in custody," she exclaimed victoriously.

"Great, you finally did some actual work," Gaby said unenthusiastically.

"That's not all. I need you ladies to testify for the jury," Jackson notified them.

"Fine, call or send it in writing. Have a nice day," Camila said, walking away.

"Wait, I need to discuss what happened at my place," Jackson yelled.

Camila turned and walked up close to Jackson. "I've never been to your place," she said, looking directly into her eyes.

They stared at each other unusually long, and Gaby fidgeted with her nails thinking Camila was entirely unhinged.

Then Camila walked off after the long stare down, and Jackson didn't stop her. "What's gotten into her?" Jackson asked Gaby once Camila turned the corner.

"I don't know, but I suggest you leave her alone. She's going through a lot," Gaby said empathetically.

"So, what's your explanation about what happened in my house?" Jackson pushed for answers.

"Lady, I've never been to your house either. So, I don't know what you're talking about," she stated, walking toward her home.

"Oh, so y'all just gonna make me look crazy?" Jackson yelled out.

"No, you're doing that all by yourself," Gaby replied smugly, shutting the door and leaving her standing outside.

Camila's mother wanted to come out and question Agent Jackson but was distracted by the phone ringing, and when she returned to look outside, Jackson was gone.

Wow, my girls did that. I'm disappointed that Mama Bear is still in the dark about everything, but Camila stuck to her guns and performed with conviction, and Gaby had her back.

They say anger is wrong, but sometimes, it's the spark we need to start a fire, and I feel my girl has set herself ablaze, speaking her mind and taking no shit.

The girls have begun classes at NYU but only cordially addressed each other. Gaby made some new acquaintances, but Camila decided to stick to herself.

Camila enjoyed commuting into the city. She enjoys people-watching, imagining what stories, traumas, love, and adventures each face concealed. She learned to recognize the pain in others' suffering and always tried to share a smile.

Gaby had been hanging out with classmates, going to movies, restaurants, and parks, and often wished Camila were there but also liked this newfound independence.

When we have long relationships, we don't realize that we develop codependence and frequently lose our identity, not knowing who we are outside those bounds.

Unfortunately, a few weeks later, Gaby received news that her grandmother had passed away while residing in the Bronx.

It was early October, and the weather had chilled. The leaves changed colors and littered everywhere, but it's still my favorite season. Halloween was just around the corner.

Camila had been frequenting her favorite spot in Central Park since the fall foliage was a magnificent sight to behold.

One evening after returning home, her father informed her that he would support Gaby's family through these challenging times.

"I don't know what's going on between you and Gaby, but I suggest you fix it. She's like family," he told Camila sternly.

Parents know everything. Even if they don't speak about it, they know. Anyone with a little common sense would see something was wrong with Camila and Gaby because they had been attached at the hip since they met.

Still, I don't think he should coerce her into rekindling her relationship with Gaby. However, Camila can still be supportive.

Customarily, parents want to impose their will on children, causing anxiety, which was happening with Camila.

I'm not a parent, so I'm not one to speak, but I know what it was like growing up with parents that suffocated by enforcing their will. It's their way or the highway, and you're often left feeling invalidated.

I'm sure they'll figure it out. Luckily, Paulo is my informant. He kept me up to speed, and I sent a flower arrangement from Carmen and me to Gaby and her family, showing our solidarity during this difficult time.

Gaby received our sympathy, peace lily/grand gardenia arrangement, and cried. That wasn't my intention.

I wanted this gesture to demonstrate that I have no hard feelings and think of her constantly while missing them dearly.

I awoke early the morning of the funeral and headed toward the kitchen when I caught Carmen sneaking out of Lazaro's room and stopped dead in my tracks. She was stunned and stared at me like a deer caught in headlights.

"Getting your groove back?" I asked, laughing because I didn't understand why she kept it from me. After all, you know what they say … if you got caught once, you've done it before.

"Ay, it's been a sad month," she said, hurrying to her room.

I chuckled and shook my head as I entered the kitchen and fetched the coffeepot. I looked out the window as I rinsed it out. The sun was beaming. It's a beautiful day, and I hope it will cheer up Gaby's mourning family.

Later, Carmen walked into the kitchen, shamefaced.

"Oh, stop behaving like an adolescent," I said, swatting her with the dish towel.

She blushed and elbowed my arm. "You know I've always had a weakness for chocolate Lacho," she grinned.

"Whatever floats your boat and tickles his pickle is not my business, Stella. So, get your groove back, girl," I said through laughter.

"You promised we'd go to the funeral today. I hope you haven't changed your mind. You need to be there for Gaby," she told me in a serious tone now.

"Of course, I'll be there. *We* will be there," I assured her.

The boys were home for the weekend and would be there, and I'm glad I will see them all if Camila shows up.

I wore a black suit and Carmen a black dress. "Wait," Carmen said, running back to her room. "I forgot my shades," she said, returning with some black sunglasses reminding me of Jackson.

I laughed at the sight. Now that Ms. Thing got her groove back, she acts like a diva.

"What?" she asked as I stared.

"Nothing, sunshine. Let's go, or we'll be late," I said and escorted her downstairs.

We arrived at the church and found it filled with family, friends, and neighbors, many of whom were sad and crying.

"Idelfonsa, Carmen, you made it," Paulo greeted us with hugs and looked handsome in a black suit.

"You clean up nicely," I told him, and he gave me a warm smile.

Thiago made his way to where we stood and hugged us tightly. He wore black pants and a black shirt.

Thiago, Carmen, and I remained seated at the rear, giving the family space. Paulo left us to join Gaby, I assumed. I looked around but didn't see Camila.

I spotted Paulo with Gaby sitting up front with her parents wearing all black. Her father looked distraught, and her mother was rubbing his back consolingly.

The church was small, with beautiful stained-glass windows and a high ceiling. A crucified Christ hung above the altar with a heavenly gaze, a solitary blood tear on his face, and his sorrow depicted the mood in the sanctuary.

A few minutes later, Camila arrived with her parents. She saw us and waved. We all waved, including Thiago.

She wore a black jumpsuit with a white blazer, and I noticed she didn't seem as radiant as usual. Instead, her aura had dimmed, making me nostalgic for when she and Gaby would walk into my shop and light it up, two stars orbiting each other.

She wore her sadness on her sleeve, obscuring her essence, which was consumed by it. It didn't suit her. I prayed she would come back to herself soon.

I watched them for a long time and found it difficult to stay. I struggled with the urge to run out. Gaby was devastated by this awful loss, and Camila was merely a shell of her former self. All of this was disheartening.

I teared up, and Carmen held my hand. I watched Thiago gazing in Camila's direction and held back a shriek. I want to stand and shout at the top of my lungs, "Enough, already!"

Instead, I sat there and allowed my emotions to take over. Everyone was sad. Everyone was crying. Maybe it's the empath in me absorbing the despair, but it felt good to release it.

We have all been miserable, and being in the same space has triggered something because Thiago had silent tears on his face. I took his hand. I wanted him to know I'm here for him … for all of them.

I was just thankful that Carmen was here for me. Unfortunately, we often must be strong for others, but no one is there for us.

The service was heartrending, and when Gaby's father spoke, everyone was in tears. Gaby was sobbing in her seat. Her mother lovingly held her close and kissed her head.

Once the service concluded, we gathered outside. Carmen and I waited for Gaby. Thiago was still with us when Camila came over to say hello.

"How are you, my dear?" I asked as I tightly embraced her.

She nodded with tears still in her eyes, and Carmen pulled her in for a hug. "Come here, you," she said.

"Hey, Camila," Thiago said once Carmen released her, and Camila went in for a hug.

Thiago was caught off guard and flailed his arms at first, but then he embraced her, and they held until Paulo arrived to interrupt.

"What's up, gang?" he asked amiably, happy to see Camila and Thiago on better terms.

Gaby joined us. "Thanks for coming," she said timidly.

"Bring it in, girl," Carmen said with outstretched arms, and Gaby leaned in for the embrace.

"We are sorry for your loss," Carmen told her.

"Yes, my sincerest condolences, Gaby," I said, and she turned and wrapped me in a bear hug.

"Thanks for being here. I'm sorry about everything," Gaby said through tears.

"Oh, honey, don't be sorry. None of it was your fault," I told her as I wiped away the tears.

"How about you all come by tomorrow? We can catch up, and I'll make sorullitos de maíz,[72] bacalaítos,[73] and all your favorites," Carmen said.

They looked at one another and nodded in agreement, and Carmen clasped her hands and jumped up with exhilaration.

"Great!" I said and then tapped Carmen's shoulder. "We are at a funeral, not a pep rally," I murmured in her ear.

---

[72] Deep-fried cornmeal sticks.
[73] Fried codfish fritters.

"See you all tomorrow," I said, and they waved as Carmen and I left. Gaby and Paulo quickly walked away, leaving Thiago and Camila alone.

"So, how's MIT?" Camila asked him bashfully.

"It's all right, but I want it to be over already," he told her.

"What? You just got there," she said, surprised.

"Yeah, well, I'm already over it," he admitted.

"That sucks," she said, looking down at her feet.

If this girl doesn't look up at Thiago, I'll scream. Camila needs to get her fire back because I'm too through with this nonsense. Sorry, let us continue.

"Life sucks," he said, and now she looked at him.

"You should be enjoying yourself, making the best of these years. If not, you'll regret it later," Camila told him.

"Too late. There's a lot I regret now," he told her coldly.

"Camila," her mother called.

"It was nice to see you. You probably don't care or want to hear it, but I'll always love you, and I miss you," Camila said and ran over to her parents before he could reply.

It felt like a slap with a bucket of ice water, and he stood there paralyzed. Then he felt the rage take over.

So why'd you leave then, huh, if you love me so damn much? he thought, his fists and teeth clenched as he fought back the tears.

I want to insert what I think here, but I'm too busy screaming, so I'll carry on because this story isn't about me. I'm just telling you how it happened.

His twin senses were jolting. Thiago needed help, so Paulo rushed over. "Hey, man, you ready to roll?" he asked Thiago wanting to get him out of there.

"You leaving?" Gaby came over to ask.

"Yeah, baby, going to take the bro home, but I'll be at your place later," Paulo told her.

"OK, bye, Gogo. Thanks for coming," she said to Thiago, who waved wordlessly.

Gogo is what Paulo called Thiago as a toddler, unable to say his name, and when Gaby found out, she started affectionately calling him that, but it's been years since she's addressed him that way.

Camila and her father argued because she refused to accompany her parents to Gaby's house.

"This isn't about Gaby, but think what you want. I'm still not going," she barked as she slammed the door to her room.

"*Es él muchacho ése, dejala*,"[74] her mother told her dad suppliantly.

She was secretly glad they broke up because now, Camila could focus on school and spend more time at home.

"*Coño, qué jodío muchacho ni muchacho. Qué sé ponga a estudiar*,"[75] her father said heatedly and stormed out.

I'm uncertain they will show up the following day, but don't discourage Carmen. She was up early, prepping in the kitchen, listening to La India singing.

"Need a hand?" I asked, hoping she'd say no.

"Nah, I'm OK," she said, knowing I don't like to cook.

"Be a doll and get me a beer," she requested, and I hurried to the fridge to fulfill the order. I must keep the chef happy.

Paulo texted Camila to ask if she wanted to ride with them to my place, and surprisingly, she accepted. "I offered Camila a ride, and she said yes. I hope you don't mind," Paulo said to Thiago.

"I don't care," he replied, shrugging his shoulders, but deep down, he got excited.

That's the thing about love. It will turn you into a full-blown masochist. He was bitter, angry, and crying yesterday, and now, today, he's excited to see the root cause of his despair.

Heart matters are hard to comprehend. It's better to feel than try to make sense of it, or we are guaranteed to lose our minds.

---

[74]   It's that boy. Leave her.
[75]   Damn, what fucking boy. What she needs to do is study.

EPISODE FOURTEEN

Paulo pulled into the driveway between the girls' houses and waited for them. Thiago rode in the front seat because he didn't want to sit in the back with Camila.

He, in fact, very much wants to, but his ego won't allow it. Then finally, the girls came out, and, of course, Gaby wouldn't make this smooth sailing.

She wore a short denim dress and high-top sneakers, with large gold hoop earrings and hot-pink lips. Her tight curls were growing in, and she looked fabulous.

"I don't care that this is your car, but I'm sitting next to my man, so get out," Gaby told Thiago, opening the passenger-side door and awaiting his exit.

Thiago gave her a nasty look but obeyed her and sat in the back next to Camila. "Thanks for the ride," Camila said.

As Thiago preferred, she had curly hair and wore blue jeans and a light blue crop-top blouse with boots. Blue was Camila's favorite color.

"No problem, sis," Paulo said, and Thiago grunted.

Maybe it's because he doesn't want Paulo to consider Camila a sister anymore. Anyhow, he didn't say a word the rest of the ride. Gaby and Paulo talked, and Camila distractedly looked out the car window.

When they arrived, Carmen was overjoyed. "They came!" she exclaimed happily.

"Thanks for coming," I said as they walked in.

"We're happy to be here. We've missed you, ladies," Paulo said.

"Let's go upstairs," Carmen said enthusiastically. She had prepared a banquet for them.

She made something for everyone—Brazilian lemonade for the boys. The condensed milk is the ingredient that sets it apart—made with fresh limes. Arepas for Gaby, sancocho for Camila, and her Puerto Rican specialties, as she'd promised.

Yes, she cooked all that food. Imagine what she will do for Thanksgiving! They all dug in, and immediately the mood changed. Everyone appeared happier.

Suddenly, someone banged on the door.

"I'll get it," I said, holding Carmen back. She was already on her feet.

You will be in disbelief when I tell you who was at the door. "We're closed on Sundays," I said, letting her in.

"I have a serious emergency," a frantic Jackson told me with a grave face. She was all business in a royal blue suit with black loafer shoes.

"You're the police!" I said to her with my hands on my hips and shaking my head. If *she* needed help, where does that leave the rest of us?

She was shaking her head too.

"Girl, you need spiritual work? Because I told you we are closed," I maintained.

"No, there's a hostage situation at a Payomatic check-cashing place near Times Square. I need the super friends," she said, looking around with crazy eyes.

"They can't help you," I said, sensing her urgency.

"Let *them* make that call," she said, staring me down.

"I would've gone directly to them, but Camila doesn't want me to come near her house," she told me with urgency.

"Oh, so if I tell you to stay away from my house, you won't come?" I asked.

"Time is of the essence, Idelfonsa. Lives are at stake. Can you get them here or not?" she asked earnestly.

I realized this was a serious matter, and I told her to wait there. Then I went upstairs to ask the girls if they were OK with seeing her. If not, I'd send her away.

It appeared that since Carmen is Alfred, I'm Gordon.

I climbed the stairs in haste because Jackson was tapping her foot and looking at her watch.

"You ladies will not believe who is looking for you," I told the girls once in the kitchen.

"Oh, hell no," Carmen said, rolling her eyes in disgust.

"Jackson?" Camila asked, getting out of her seat.

"Yup," I said as I removed empty plates in front of them.

"What does she want? Gaby is going through a lot right now; actually, we all are," Paulo said protectively, looking over at Thiago and Camila.

"Something about a hostage situation, but if you guys don't want to see her, I'll ask her to leave," I said.

"I'll dismiss her," Camila stated, walking out of the kitchen.

"Well, let's just hear her out," Gaby said with curiosity, following Camila.

In collective agreement, the others stood and marched downstairs to see this urgent situation that caused Jackson to disturb us on a Sunday.

"Look, the gang is all back together," she said, seeing us smiling like kids in a candy store.

"Make this quick," Camila told her as she finished descending the stairs.

Gaby stood so close to Camila that I didn't think you could pass a sheet of paper between them.

"Trust me; I will. Unfortunately, there's a hostage situation, and a violent man has threatened a child's life," she said earnestly to them.

Gaby looked over at Camila. *What does that have to do with us? What does she expect us to do? We don't have any superpowers*, Gaby thought.

I don't know. Jackson is crazy, Camila thought.

Jackson stared at them, wondering if they were doing the "telepathy thing," but she didn't ask. She didn't want to piss them off and risk getting rejected.

"What is it you want from them?" I asked, trying to get this show on the road because I knew she must have some crazy proposition.

"I need them to teleport into the room where the boy is being held and get him out," she declared.

We all looked at one another in disbelief. Was this woman out of her mind? She expected the girls to risk their lives and expose themselves? What if this madman killed them in the process?

"No, have a blessed day," I said before Camila wanted to put on the imaginary cape and save the day.

Jackson pleadingly looked at the girls one last time, then despondently turned to leave. The clock was ticking, and she realized she had come here only to waste her precious time.

"Wait," Camila said … and we all looked at her.

Here we go! I wish Jackson had run out the door because once this girl's wheels start turning, it's a wrap. I hope you understand what I mean.

Jackson ran back to face Camila. "What guarantee do you have for us? I will not expose Gaby and me. How can you promise we'll be safe?" she asked Jackson.

"It's a need to know and classified, but there is a small window in that room protected by a gate. My people are working on getting the gate off, but it's a small space only the boy can fit in. However, he's too small to reach it. So the only way to get him out is to have someone on the inside help him. So that's where you two come in," she explained.

I don't know. My gut is telling me this is a bad idea. Why enlist the help of two young girls? You want to extract the hostage, not send in two more potential hostages. I'm sure the FBI can find a way that doesn't involve Camila and Gabriela. Jackson saw the apprehension and elaborated on the plan.

"He's two years old, so your secret will be safe. We will throw a harness in and pull him out, but we know he can't figure it out on his own because he's so young. So, all you have to do is get in there, secure him in the harness, and we'll do the rest," Jackson said persuasively.

"You'll be his guardian angels. He can't speak yet. So then you ladies get out, and no one will know you were ever there," she continued convincingly.

"Fine," Camila told her definitively.

"Um, it's a party of two, and I didn't see the other party agree to this madness," Paulo interjected.

"I'll do it," Gaby decided.

"What?" Paulo asked disbelievingly.

"Have you two lost your minds? You can get killed!" Thiago added.

"Oh well, life sucks. Isn't that what you said, Thiago? So, what do you care?" Camila asked him bitterly.

We were all confused about what they meant, but Jackson looked at Thiago like she didn't care what he thought and was glad Camila was on board.

"OK, go on your suicide mission. You're right. I don't care," Thiago stated, leaving. Camila wanted to stop him but didn't.

Don't leave me. I need you, Camila thought as she watched Thiago go out the door.

"We are wasting time here, people," Jackson stated.

"Everyone, calm down," Carmen said with arms raised.

"Girls, are you sure you want to do this?" she asked Camila and Gaby.

"Yes," they answered simultaneously.

"OK, then, this is very brave and honorable of you, ladies, but make sure you have a plan, and if something happens to them, I will beat your ass," Carmen said, turning to face Jackson.

Jackson nodded in acknowledgment, and Carmen gave her a crooked smile.

"We're running out of time. So let's go, and I'll go over everything in the car, and you can tell me how this works on your end," Jackson said, heading for the door.

"Tell us the name of the place and the exact location we need to be. The rest is a need to know," Camila said to her.

Jackson looked over at Camila and smiled. "Touché," she said.

"I'm coming too," Paulo declared, running after them.

"Hurry up, Romeo," Jackson told him.

They jumped into the SUV Jackson was driving, and she peeled out fast.

"Listen, the truth is no one knows you'll be there, you'll wait in my car, and when it's 'go time,' I'll text you. You go in, secure the kid, and get out. Then once you let me know you got it done, I'll have him hoisted to safety, *comprende?*"[76] she asked them.

"Yes," they said, and Paulo shook his head.

---

[76] Understand?

"You make it sound so easy," he told Jackson, uneasy.

"It's supposed to be. It *will* be!" she said confidently.

Camila sat there thinking this was why she was supposed to reveal their secret to Jackson so that they could be of assistance in cases like these.

All of you already know what I'm going to say, but if she wants to play the superhero, I'll support her—even if I don't like it.

They arrived at the scene. Police were everywhere, and the entire area was on lockdown. A helicopter hovered overhead, and police dogs were sniffing around.

The media was there, and reporters were covering the incident live. One female reporter took one last look in her mirror before the camera rolled.

"Live from Times Square. A suspect has a check-cashing place terrorized as he holds five people hostage, including a two-year-old boy he has taken from the mother and locked in a room," she reported from across the street.

"Okay, stay here. I'll let you know when to go in. Good thing you came, Romeo, because I don't want them using a phone there, so you tell me when they're there. I want you ladies in and out. I'll know we can move when you're back out, OK?" she asked, storing Paulo's number in her phone.

"Where's the boy?" Camila asked.

"It's that Payomatic," Jackson pointed across the street. "He's in the storage room. There's only one," Jackson told her.

"Got it," Camila acknowledged.

"Good luck," Jackson said as she shut the vehicle door.

"Please, be careful, and just so you know, Thiago would die if something happened to you, Camila," Paulo told her.

"You better die too if something happens to me because if I die, *you* die. You ain't gonna be out here with another girl while I'm dead," Gaby teased him.

Paulo laughed. "No one could ever fill your shoes or take your place, my love. I love you," he said, kissing her.

Camila looked away, wishing Thiago were there. She regretted what she said, and if she was about to die, none of what had happened mattered anyway.

I wish I could tell him I love him and kiss him one last time, she thought while trembling with fear.

We need to slow down and think before opening our big mouths because things we feel are a big deal turn out to be trivial when confronted with something of this magnitude. Life is short. We need to love deeply, laugh often, and count our blessings.

"*Ave Maria*,[77] I can't take it. Did Paulo text you?" Carmen asked, and I heard a tap on the door.

"They're back!" Carmen screamed as I rushed to the door with Midnight at my heels.

It was Thiago. "Hey, I just needed some air," he said as he walked in.

"Where's Paulo?" he asked, looking around.

"He went with them," I said as I pulled a stool for Thiago to sit. He had on ripped jeans, a white T-shirt, and white sneakers.

"Oh," he said, sitting, and I turned on a small TV mounted on the wall.

They were reporting live from the scene. I scrutinized the image expecting to see Jackson in the background, but I didn't and instead focused on Thiago.

"How are you, Thiago?" I asked. I think he should talk about it. Men are so accustomed to bottling up their emotions, and I knew it was unhealthy.

"I've been better," he said, aimlessly scribbling on a notepad on the counter.

"How are you coping with the breakup?" I asked directly.

Sometimes, we need to be direct. For example, if you know someone you care about is struggling with something, asking how you are doing won't cut it because people will lie and say they're OK.

"It's killing me, Idely," he said, looking up at me.

I went over and placed my hand on his shoulder. "Thiago, I know this is difficult, and I know you're angry, but don't give up. If you love

---

[77] Hail Mary

Camila, honor her wishes but don't give up. You know she loves you, which should be enough to make you fight for it," I said.

"It's hard, though," he said sadly.

"Son, nothing good ever comes easy. The world is full of people in love who are not together because we are all too lazy, scared, or weak to fight for love. We easily engage in hatred but show cowardice in the face of love. The gutless don't deserve true love," I said with melancholy.

"I don't know what to do. What *can* I do?" he asked desperately.

"Don't coward away, don't desert her; just continue to be her friend. Talk to her, not condescendingly, not bitterly, but with love. Continue to love her. If she's no longer your girlfriend, it's OK. True love is unconditional. You appear to have had a condition of physical intimacy, and now that she has withdrawn it, you're upset, right?"

"It's not even like that. We spent most of our relationship without sex," he argued.

"I know. I only want you to look within yourself and find the condition so you can eliminate it. Could it be that it's about possession? Because she's no longer yours, you think she can be another's, which makes you bitter?" I asked him.

He was quiet for a long time, probably considering what I'd said. It's a lot to ponder, but I hope he does.

Love shouldn't be a cage. We should give the object of our affection wings to fly with the confidence that they will continue to choose us every time, or in his case, it will return to him.

"It's not like she left you for someone else. Then I'd understand why you're so upset," I said after a while.

"Shit, I'd be bitter too," Carmen reinforced.

"She left you for herself. Just switch gears and be there as a loving friend. When she's ready to share herself again, be there to swoop back into your old position. But if you distance yourself, someone else will come and take the spot," I told him, and Carmen winked at him.

"*Mijo,*[78] listen to those words of wisdom. I wish she had been this wise when we were young. It would've saved me a lot of heartaches," Carmen said, and he gave us a handsome dimpled smile.

---

[78] Son

Instantly, I felt him shift and sit up taller with more confidence. I hope that's what he needed to get out of this rut.

If life gives you lemons, juggle those suckers and put on a show, but don't sit back and let life bully you into submission. This life is only for the brave.

Find someone to confide in and talk about what troubles you. Don't let sadness and depression eat you alive. Often, a little advice will make a big difference and allow you to see things from a different perspective.

Thiago took his phone from his back pocket. I love you, Camila De Los Santos, and I'll always be here for you. I'm sorry if I've been a bad friend. I was struggling being your ex-boyfriend. Please come back to me safely. I need you, he wrote and smiled.

Carmen and I smiled at each other, and let me tell you this … It takes a tribe. So, be a mentor and friend to those you find along your journey through life.

Camila's phone buzzed, and she looked over at Gaby, ready to go, but it was a text from Thiago. She read it a few times. I love you too! she replied with a smile.

"OK, you're a go," Paulo told them nervously.

Camila and Gaby held hands and disappeared. Paulo was so scared for them that he started to pray.

They popped up in the room where the child was alone. Their fear was so intense that their knees buckled, and they fell to the ground.

The boy hysterically cried, his face wet with mucus and tears. He was hyperventilating from fear. Camila quickly went over to fetch the harness. Next, they heard a noise outside and gasped.

Hurry up, Gaby thought, frightened.

Camila nodded. She was so incredibly terrified she couldn't formulate her thoughts, and her hands uncontrollably shook as she secured the boy onto the harness.

They heard another loud sound outside the door, and Gaby clasped her chest. *Let's get out of here*, she thought pleadingly.

We should wait for him to be out before we go. We can't just leave him, Camila thought.

"Camila, we have strict instructions. Jackson will not pull him out until we are out. The sooner we leave, the faster he's out," Gaby told her, yanking her hand and squeezing it tightly.

Meanwhile, Thiago was pacing, and Carmen was tapping a pen on the counter, which wasn't very reassuring, so I asked her to stop. We'd been glued to the television for about an hour and still hadn't received a word from Paulo.

Jackson said it was supposed to be a quick extraction—in and out—so what could be taking this long?

"What is taking so long?" Thiago asked anxiously.

"I know. Paulo should be giving us up-to-date reports," Carmen said, nervously tapping her foot.

"Paulo is probably in worse shape than we are. So, let's remain calm," I said, sounding cool.

Suddenly, someone knocked on the door unexpectedly, and it startled me so much that I jumped up, letting out a yelp. "For the love of God!" I screamed as I rushed to the door.

"That was nerve-racking," said a fidgety Paulo crossing the threshold. "This stress level can't be healthy," he continued walking up to Thiago.

"We survived!" exclaimed Gaby walking in, and the sight of her provided instant relief.

"That was the scariest thing I've done in my life. I was sure that psycho would walk in, and, well, I can't even say it," Camila said, locking the door behind her.

Thiago ran over and hugged Camila. "I'm so glad you're OK," he said to her.

"Where's Jackson?" Carmen asked.

"She had to stay. There are still hostages to rescue," Gaby said.

"Won't that demon be furious when he finds out the kid is gone and hurt the other hostages?" I asked.

"Listen, I'm just glad we got out of there. We took a taxi back, and it was a nightmare because the police had streets closed all over the place, creating terrible traffic jams. So getting back here was a real mission," Paulo informed us.

"Jackson said they weren't going to tell him the boy was out. They will still meet the demands and get everyone out safely. She simply didn't want the child in there alone," Camila told us.

"Whatever. You guys did your part. I'm very proud of you ladies," Carmen said, relieved.

"Now, let's go up so I can make some chamomile tea, and we can finish watching the events unfold on TV," I told them, and we hurried upstairs.

EPISODE FIFTEEN

The kids have returned to school, and Carmen and I were looking forward to Thanksgiving break. We have a Friendsgiving Dinner planned, and Carmen can hardly wait. She has a list of everything she'll be cooking and has been preparing for weeks.

"I'm going to cook a feast. The kids will love it. It'll be great," she exclaimed from the register as she wrote more items on her list of ingredients.

"Yes, they will, and so will I," I told her happily as I restocked some merchandise.

Camila and Gaby were on better terms, but things weren't like before. Gaby had a new friend, Chantrea Sok, a beautiful young lady with short, silky black hair, tanned skin, and dark brown round eyes. Her family immigrated from Cambodia when she was two years old.

Thiago had spent a lot of time with his study partner, Diya Patel, a stunning Indian girl with long, honeyed hair, beautiful dark skin, and striking, upturned hazel eyes. He and Camila texted regularly, and he no longer felt so angry about their breakup.

"Hey," Gaby said when Camila left her house on her way to school one morning.

"Hey," Camila replied.

"Can I roll to school with you today? I have an early class too," Gaby asked.

"Sure," Camila replied, feeling wary about Gaby's sudden desire to go to school with her.

They headed toward the bus stop on the sidewalk. It was early and unseasonably cold, so Gaby wrapped a scarf around her neck as Camila zipped up her coat.

"You know Paulo told me that Thiago has spent a lot of time with some girl," Gaby told her, sounding casual.

There it was. Gaby proved Camila's suspicion right. I didn't understand Gaby's need to bring this up.

"Yes, Diya. I know. He's told me about her," Camila said, irked, feeling the only reason Gaby wanted to go to school with her was to gossip about Thiago.

"Oh, that's nice. You two have managed to save your friendship, but doesn't it bother you that Thiago has another girlfriend already?" Gaby questioned.

Now, Camila was upset. *She doesn't give a shit about me. She only wants to rub this in my face*, she thought.

"I only care that Thiago is back to being himself and is happy," Camila told Gaby dryly.

"Girl, stop playing yourself and go get your man. Don't let another chick have him so easily," Gaby suggested.

"I broke up with Thiago for this reason so that he can be free to do as he pleases without me having to worry about it. Now that he's happy and moving on, I'm not going to try to get him back. That's not 'go get your man.' That's selfish, bitch," a stirred Camila said to Gaby.

"If I were you, I'd get him back. That breakup was pointless," Gaby said, pressing more of Camila's buttons.

"Well, you're *not* me, and it's none of your business," Camila stated, and they continued the rest of the trip without speaking.

When they arrived at school, Chantrea was waiting outside for Gaby. "Hey, girl," she said, running up to Gaby. "You're not going to believe who called me last night," Chantrea continued giddily.

Camila walked on, leaving Gaby with her new friend. She was glad that Chantrea saved her from further interaction with Gaby, and Gaby watched Camila disappear inside the building, feeling sad.

"Who?" Gaby asked as they walked toward the university building.

Paulo sent Gaby his usual morning text, "Good morning, beautiful. Miss you like the air I breathe," he wrote.

Thiago was already at the library with Diya. "Hey, you want to see *Breaking Dawn* Part 2 tonight?" Diya asked.

"Um, I thought I'd go with my girlfriend, ex, I mean, friend, over Thanksgiving break," Thiago said clumsily.

"You mean Camila, the one who dumped you for no reason?" Diya asked him, amused.

"Yes, the very same one," he answered, embarrassed.

"Thiago, you and I are friends. I'm not asking you on a date, and here's some friendly advice. Don't put your life on hold for people who don't want you in theirs," she said, shoving him lightly.

"Ouch," he said with a grimace.

"So, that's settled. We'll watch this movie tonight. I won't take no for an answer," Diya insisted.

"Yes, ma'am," Thiago obliged.

The kids have gone their separate ways. Meeting new people was bound to happen. So perhaps Camila was right all along.

After her classes at NYU, Camila went to the cell phone store. Unfortunately, the cheap phone she purchased months back had stopped working.

"Hey, nice to see you again," Andres said when she reached the counter.

"This crap stopped working," she whined, handing him her cell phone.

"I'm sorry to hear that," he told her, taking it. "You look beautiful, by the way. That blue shirt suits you well," he said, and Camila blushed.

"Thank you," she replied bashfully, pushing her curls behind her ears.

"Will you be getting a new phone or sending this one out for repair?" he asked her with a smile.

"I'll get the newest you have, please," she replied, smiling.

"One new phone coming right up," he said animatedly.

Camila giggled as she waited for Andres to retrieve her new phone. Next, she grabbed a case and placed it on the counter. The shop was empty.

Camila's curly hair was out, gloriously adorning her head like a crown.

"So, do you have a boyfriend or something?" Andres asked.

"Um, no," she said sadly.

"Bad breakup, huh?" he inquired, sensing her mood change.

"Something like that," she admitted.

"You'll get over it, I promise," he encouraged her with another radiant smile.

Andres was a charming boy with pale skin, golden-brown hair, and light brown eyes.

"Where are you from?" he asked as he inserted the sim card into her new phone.

"Yonkers," Camila replied, laughing.

"Beautiful *and* funny," he said, laughing too.

"Wait, isn't that what you wanted to know?" Camila teased.

"And smart, but I meant ethnicity," he added.

"Oh, African!" Camila exclaimed and burst out laughing this time.

Andres laughed too. "Where in Africa?" he asked, leaning on the counter, resting his chin in his palm, and staring at her.

Camila shifted uncomfortably on her feet with his intense gaze upon her. "The Dominican Republic," she exclaimed with nervous laughter.

"Excuse me, miss, but you've just failed geography," Andres told her, amused, as he got back to setting up her new phone.

They both giggled as she handed him her card so that he could complete the order.

"That's cool. My stepdad is Dominican, a funny dude, but my parents are both from Venezuela, in case you were wondering," he said, giving Camila back her card.

"I was, so thanks for clarifying that for me," she said, taking her card and the bag where he carefully packed the box for the phone and the accessories she had just purchased.

"I see your phone number here in the system. Is it OK if I use it to contact you? Since the first time I met you, I gave you my number, and you never used it," he said to her, hopeful.

"Sure, Andres, I could use a new friend," she told him and walked out of the store.

The others were all moving on, meeting new people, and doing new things. Perhaps Camila should also do the same.

Finally, Thanksgiving break arrived, the boys were home, and Gaby was thrilled Paulo had come to visit a few times, but she felt it was not enough.

Also, she held some resentment toward Camila. The two could've seen the guys as much as they wanted with their abilities, but Camila had to ruin everything.

"Hey, baby," Gaby said, running outside to greet Paulo. He lifted her in the air, and she wrapped her legs around his waist as she passionately kissed him.

"I've missed you," he said, putting her down.

"I've missed you more," she told him, giving him a tight squeeze.

"Let's go," he said.

Paulo received cash as a graduation gift, and Thiago got a car, making everything better for them. Finally, they had space to do their own thing.

"Why didn't you guys just carpool?" Gaby asked Paulo, getting into the car.

"Bro has been doing his own thing. He even went on a date to the movies with Diya, and they watched the new *Twilight* flick," Paulo informed her.

"That is sinful. We watched all those movies together. How could Thiago go watch it with someone else?" Gaby asked, hurt.

"Babe, you and I will see it together. That's *all* that matters. Thiago and Camila broke up. So, let it go," he said.

"Oh my God, where is the Time Thief? Time is flying by. I can't believe it's our Friendsgiving Dinner already," Carmen said, still busy in the kitchen.

"Relax, Nena. Everything will be perfect. I can't believe you made coquito like it's Christmas," I said, tickled.

"Oh, I'll make more for the holidays, you'll see," she replied, taking the pasteles[79] out of the refrigerator.

---

[79] Pork, chicken, or beef, and adobo stuffing wrapped in plantain masa and wrapped in banana leaves.

I chuckled, knowing she certainly will. Then finally, I heard the doorbell and went to open it.

"How are you, Idely?" Thiago asked, coming in.

"Where are the others?" I said, looking outside, and saw Camila walking over.

"Paulo went to pick up Gaby. I assume Camila is on her way," he replied right as Camila entered.

"You assumed correctly," she said, smiling and warmly hugging me.

"Hey, you," Thiago said, hugging Camila.

"Nice to see you," Camila told him.

"Yeah, same," he said, and before I could shut the door, Paulo pulled up and parked in front.

"Everyone is here!" I happily exclaimed as Gaby jumped out and hurried over to embrace me.

"You live nearby and never stop by anymore," I said to Gaby reproachfully.

"I've been super busy with school, and the commute is killing me. I should've dormed there," Gaby told me apologetically.

"I understand," I said, squeezing her.

Camila stopped by from time to time to say hello, maybe because she hadn't been able to make new friends. The thought of that saddened me. I like that she visits, but I'd like it more if she were enjoying herself at her new school.

Paulo and Camila hugged, and I told them to get upstairs because Carmen was anxiously awaiting their arrival.

"Yayy!" Carmen exclaimed when she saw them. "I deep-fried a turkey, made some arroz con guandules,[80] baked a chicken and ham, and made a potato salad, green salad, pasteles,[81] empanadas, white rice, lasagna, and flan," she told them excitedly.

"I made a pumpkin pie," I said, and we all laughed.

"You made … or you *bought*?" Paulo asked playfully.

"The point is, there is pumpkin pie," I laughed.

---

[80] Rice and peas

[81] Pork, chicken, or beef, and adobo stuffing wrapped in plantain masa and wrapped again in banana leaves.

Carmen beautifully set the table with festive plates and napkins depicting a turkey, pumpkin, and autumn leaves. There was also a large fruit bowl filled with oranges, apples, and grapes.

I took out one of Carmen's many coquito bottles and served a glass to everyone. "A toast," I said, and we raised our glasses.

"To friends that became family. Let us never take our bond for granted, and let the love we feel for one another endure the tests of life. And though we travel different paths on our journeys, may we always find our way back to one another," I said with tears.

"Amen," Carmen said, wiping tears from her eyes.

"Cheers," the kids said, drinking their coquito.

We feasted, laughed, and talked about what we'd been up to, but things got awkward when Gaby added a little more than she should've.

"Thiago, tell us about your new girlfriend," she tactlessly said.

He looked at her, puzzled. "I don't recall telling you I have a new girlfriend," he replied, shocked by her intrusion.

"I heard it through the grapevine," she said, taking a bite from the chicken on her plate.

Camila turned scarlet and was grilling Gaby, visibly upset. "She can't seem to mind her own business. I told her Diya was a friend when she came to me with the news, and if the two of you are dating, it's not her concern," Camila retorted.

Thiago seemed uncomfortable with the subject, and Paulo blushed guiltily. "Well, that's the last you'll be hearing from those vines," he said to Gaby.

"What's the big deal? It's not a secret. He had already told Camila about the girl. I just want to know more about her," Gaby said defensively.

"The big deal is that she's *not* my girlfriend, and it's *not* your business," Thiago stated.

"Not your girlfriend, but you went to the movies to see the new *Twilight* with her—not us," Gaby accused him.

"You're unbelievable," Camila said, standing and walking out.

Thiago stood and followed Camila downstairs.

"Cam, wait," he said, reaching for her arm.

"Thiago, before you try to explain anything, let me stop you. You've already told me about Diya, and I am sincerely happy that you're carrying on and making new friends. I don't care that you go to the movies or do whatever you do. I'm happy for you. However, this is about Gaby, not you. So go back, enjoy the rest of your evening, and please indulge her curiosity, telling her all about Diya," she told him and continued down.

"Don't go. You haven't had your supper yet," he implored.

"I've lost my appetite," she said and was gone.

He sat on one of the stairs, and I came down and sat beside him. "Maybe we're all not compatible anymore, and there is no sense in forcing these interactions. We can each visit Carmen and you individually," he said, distraught.

"Maybe you're right. But unfortunately, it appears Carmen and I want to hold on to something that is no longer there, and perhaps it's time we let go," I said to him, defeated.

"Why does everyone always take *her* side?" Gaby yelled, storming down the stairs. Thiago jumped up to get out of the way.

"Why do *you* have to be like that? There is *no side*. I'm calling you out for your lack of tact and insensitivity, but it's impossible because you always think you're right," Paulo yelled as she walked away.

"You know what, Paulo? I don't give a fuck. Maybe we need a break too. Go date Diya's best friend and carry on like Camila and I never existed," Gaby screamed, running out the door.

Oh boy, don't be hard on Gaby. She has been silently going through a lot. She acts tough, like it doesn't bother her, but Camila and Thiago's breakup has affected her too.

She felt Camila betrayed her, let her down, and was selfish, and maybe those feelings made Gaby egotistical, but she was hoping they could teleport to the dorm every night and back home in the mornings. Who can blame her?

They had been inseparable for four years, and their lives had turned upside down. It's a lot to cope with emotionally.

A break may be what they all need, time to do their own thing apart. I believe that will make the heart grow fonder.

"Come on, let's eat," Carmen said discontentedly, and we somberly followed her back upstairs.

The following day Camila was at the shop early.

"Hey, doll," I told her happily.

"Hi, Camila," Carmen said without looking up as she counted the money in the register.

"I'm sorry I walked out on dinner yesterday, I know how hard you worked to prepare all that food, and my behavior was immature and ungrateful," she said, going over to hug Carmen.

"Oh, I forgive you, little brat," Carmen replied, ruffling her hair.

"Are there any leftovers?" Camila asked, smiling.

"Of course," Carmen said happily.

"Great, I'll be upstairs having breakfast," Camila said, rushing up the stairs.

"My Lord, teenage mood swings give me whiplash," Carmen stated once she was gone.

"Tell me about it," I said, laughing.

Then, the door jingled, and Carmen and I watched Gaby sashay in, looking happy.

"Good morning, beautiful ladies," she told us.

"Good morning, I'd ask how you're holding up, but you're doing great, apparently," I said.

"Sorry about last night. I should've eaten and *then* stormed out. It was stupid of me to storm out on an empty stomach," she said, and we laughed.

"Well, there are plenty of leftovers. So, help yourself," Carmen informed her.

"It's a bit early for that, but since I went to sleep angry and hungry, and I am famished, don't mind if I do," Gaby said.

"Go eat, my dear. We'll be right here," I told her.

"Should we have told her that her best friend is up there?" Carmen asked me.

"She'll find out soon enough," I replied, and Carmen winked.

"Oh, Idely should've said you were up here," Gaby said when she saw Camila.

"Would that have kept you from coming up?" Camila asked indifferently.

"Nope, not going hungry again because of you," Gaby replied.

"Because of *me*? You've got some freaking nerve. Maybe if you learn to mind your business and shut the hell up, you wouldn't ruin everything all the time," Camila shouted at her.

"You self-righteous little bitch! How dare you tell me I ruined everything when you destroyed all our lives? We could've seen Thiago and Paulo every day. Nothing had to change, but you only thought about yourself. You're a weak little brat who couldn't handle things getting a little hard, and now you want to take it out on me," Gaby screamed back.

"Yeah, that's all I'm good for—doing what *you* want and catering to all *your* stupid ideas. That's all these fucking abilities are to you—a means to get what *you* want," Camila barked.

"Right, because you went and saved that kid all by yourself. I'm glad Thiago has a new girlfriend because you don't deserve him, and I'm glad we aren't friends anymore because you're a bitch," Gaby said with a knot in her throat.

I heard the screaming and went upstairs. I hoped the girls would make up and not pull each other's hair out.

"What the hell is going on?" I asked.

"Nothing. Camila is just a smug bitch," Gaby told me, her face red and eyes teary.

Camila didn't answer, and I took both of them by the hand.

"My grandmother used to tell me a story about two sisters, both enslaved in Cuba, and when the ten-year war began in eighteen sixty-eight, they had gotten into a terrible fight," I told them.

"Having to flee with their master's family, they ran through the woods. One sister fell behind and got captured by a group of slave rebels. Can you imagine being taken from the only family you know?" I asked them.

"A ship awaited on the beach, and she watched as they sailed away without her. They yelled and said awful things to each other. That was their goodbye, and she never saw her sister again," I said.

Camila and Gaby looked down at their feet with tears falling from their eyes.

"My grandmother told my brother and me this story every time we got into nasty arguments, and the moral of the story is that life is short, and it can change in an instant and that most of the things we argue about are silly," I said.

I wish I could be in Cuba in eighteen sixty-eight and tell those sisters to hug and forgive each other before life rips them apart, Camila thought.

I was still holding each of their hands tightly, praying they would make up.

I wish I could be in Cuba in eighteen sixty-eight to help those sisters escape together, Gaby thought, and suddenly ... the three of us disappeared!

ABOUT THE AUTHOR

J.P. Ozuna was born in the Dominican Republic and raised in the Bronx, NY. Ozuna worked for eighteen years in public service with the City of New York. An avid reader and passionate writer, she hopes to inspire her three children and future generations to follow their dreams. Author of 2030: Nothing Is What It Seems, Diaspora is her second novel. Currently, she lives with her beautiful family in Putnam County, New York.

www.platanopublishing.com

j.p.ozuna

JPOZUNA1